Pip: the Story of Olive

www.**davidficklingbooks**.co.uk

Pip:
the story of
Olive

Kim Kane

David Fickling Books

OXFORD · NEW YORK

31 Beaumont Street
Oxford OX1 2NP, UK

PIP: THE STORY OF OLIVE
A DAVID FICKLING BOOK 978 1 849 92002 5

First published in Australia by Allen and Unwin in 2008

First published in Great Britain by David Fickling Books,
a division of Random House Children's Books
A Random House Group Company

Hardback edition published 2008
This edition published 2010

1 3 5 7 9 10 8 6 4 2

Set in Cochin

DAVID FICKLING BOOKS
31 Beaumont Street, Oxford, OX1 2NP

www.kidsatrandomhouse.co.uk
www.rbooks.co.uk

Addresses for companies within The Random House Group Limited can be found at:
www.randomhouse.co.uk/offices.htm

THE RANDOM HOUSE GROUP Limited Reg. No. 954009

A CIP catalogue record for this book is available from the British Library.

Printed and bound in Great Britain by
CPI Bookmarque, Croydon, CR0 4TD

For PJS

One face, one voice, one habit, and two persons;
A natural perspective, that is, and is not.

William Shakespeare, *Twelfth Night* (v, 1, 216–17)

Contents

1
Chicken Loaf and Chaos

Olive Garnaut looked ever so slightly like an extraterrestrial: a very pale extraterrestrial. She had long thin hair, which hung and swung, and a long thin face to match it. Her eyes were pale green and so widely spaced that if she looked out of the corners of them she could actually see her plaits banging against her bottom.

Olive's eyelashes and eyebrows were so very fair that they blended right into her forehead and people could only spot them if the sun caught her at a strange angle. When she stood, her feet turned out at one hundred and sixty degrees (like a ballerina in first position), and her shins were the exact colour of chicken loaf.

It went without saying that Olive was the most peculiar-looking girl in Year 7. But what happened to Olive Garnaut was not because she looked ever so slightly like an extraterrestrial, even a very pale one.

'Yer mum go and bleach yer, did she?' said the baker every time Olive went to buy buns. 'Those arms'd burn in two minutes at the beach.' The baker always laughed and Olive always flushed puce to her hair roots.

Olive liked to buy buns six at a time, even though she knew that five would probably be tossed into the compost after they had gone splotchy in the breadbin. Olive liked the baker to think that she might just be collecting buns to take home to a family full of children and noise, a family like Mathilda Graham's.

'Mrs Graham doesn't buy her buns, she bakes them, and she certainly doesn't let them go green in the breadbin,' Olive would mutter near Mog.

'How else would penicillin have been invented?' Mog would respond (nursing a gin-and-tonic headache and willing to embrace mould). Mog was Olive's mum, and Olive called her Mog because that's the sort of family they were. But Olive called her 'Mum' at school – the same way she sometimes made her own sandwiches, rather than buying them from the tuckshop, and then pretended that Mog had prepared them instead. Olive would say, rather too loudly, 'Gross, Mum's given me cheese 'n' gherkin spread again.' Nobody took much notice – except Mathilda, who knew but didn't say anything. Mathilda Graham was Olive's best friend. Olive liked Mathilda; Mathilda liked tuck lunches.

Mathilda was one of the only friends Olive had ever brought home. Olive lived 'out in the sticks' (or so Mathilda's mum grumbled when she dropped Olive off). While Mathilda could walk to school, Olive faced a three-tram ride or a taxi. But it wasn't just distance that made Olive reluctant to bring anybody home.

Olive and Mog rattled around in a ramshackle house with five bedrooms, a drawing room, a sitting room, a morning room, two studies, a billiard room, a cellar, a scullery, and a room with no name that had bars on the windows because the family before them had collected stamps. The house was right near the sea and was Federation in style, which meant that it was built when Australia became a nation of states and women wore whalebone in their singlets to make them look thin. Mog always complained that it hadn't been touched since.

Mog liked the idea of living in a magazine house, but she didn't have the time to be neat or the patience for interior decorators. 'This home may look as weary as I feel, but it's got good bones,' she'd say. 'Besides, I have better things to do with my time than discuss whether the kitchen would look more "of the minute" painted in butter-yellow or clotted milk.'

Olive rather fancied the idea of their house with butter-yellow or clotted-milk walls. It would be like living in a cream tea, she thought. It could only be better than cobwebs and stains.

While Mog did not have time for interior decorators, she did have time to look in junk shops. On special week-ends, when Mog wasn't working, Olive and Mog travelled through the country in a hire car with a driver, trawling through second-hand shops, eating tarts and searching for gems with jammy fingers. Mog swore that she would strip the gems and turn them into something new and stylish, but they both knew, somewhere not too deep down, that she never would. Consequently, Mog and Olive had a real Colonial fridge with torn flywire; a 'Leading Lady' hairdryer; seventies dolls with nipped waists; and champagne saucers with bubbled glass, which they always meant to stack into a pyramid just like in an old Grace Kelly movie.

Perhaps their most beautiful find was the Brass Eye – an antique marble, about the size of a bubblegum ball, tucked into the tip of a hollow metal stem. It was slightly longer than a lipstick and looked like a tiny squat telescope. Mog and Olive had bought it in a shop on the goldfields from a man with a tic that made him wink.

Olive kept all the golden bits on the Brass Eye polished with Brasso and an old tennis sock. It rattled as she rubbed it. When Olive looked through the stem of the Brass Eye, the light refracted and everything appeared in triangles and circles. If she moved towards an object, Olive could see it spliced into hundreds of pieces; if she moved away, the object shot outwards, exploding from pinpoints like choreographed fireworks or synchronized swimmers. Olive liked to point the Brass Eye at her shoes and watch as her T-bars doubled, quadrupled and then octupled while she pulled back slowly, until they finally ignited in a dazzling jumble of school socks and silver buckles.

'But how *does* it work?' Olive asked Mog again and again.

'It's all smoke and mirrors, Ol,' Mog said. And, as a child, Olive had imagined that the stem of the Brass Eye rattled because it was filled with tiny mirrors and little Indians who burned wet matchsticks and wafted smoke along the brass tube; brassy smoke to multiply Olive's school socks and T-bar shoes.

Unfortunately not everything was as beautiful as the Brass Eye. When Mog and Olive returned home from their junk-hunts, Mog would put the stuff down wherever there was space – and there it would usually stay. Much to Olive's shame, the house was crowded with mountains of knick-knacks and clutter that lined the hall and cast shadows in dank piles. The piles were so high in places that she couldn't see over them, and the dust made her wheeze. Nobody at school had to live in bedlam like that.

'Mog, this chaos is *deesgusting*,' Olive would say, working her way through the mess; tick-tack-toeing along record covers.

'Chaos is merely order waiting to be decoded,' Mog would respond.

'Mrs Graham says that an untidy house shows an untidy mind,' Olive would shoot back (but only ever in a whisper). As a consequence of the mess, Olive stuck to her bedroom and the kitchen – which she always kept clutter-free and tidy-minded.

Olive liked her bedroom symmetrical. She liked things in pairs. She had two beds with matching duvets; two lampshades with sage velvet trim; and two bedside tables, each with its own box of tissues and a copy of *Anne of Green Gables*. Around the walls, Olive had strung chains of paper dolls holding hands. They were meant to look like the French schoolgirls in the *Madeline* books, but Olive didn't have a navy felt tip, so their coats were red. To make the dolls, Olive had folded the butcher's paper carefully down the centre to ensure that their heads and hats were exactly even. Two perfect halves.

Olive believed that everything had two perfect halves – that halves were somehow essential, oats in the porridge of life. In the body, for example, there are two eyes, two ears, two feet, two hands, two kidneys. Even tricky things like the nose and mouth are really comprised of twos (two nostrils, two rows of teeth). It wasn't something that Olive worried about or even discussed; just something that she had noticed ever since she'd discovered she was born at 2.22 a.m. on the second of February, weighing in at a tiny 2.2 kilograms.

'Cosmic,' WilliamPetersMustardSeed had responded (well, so Mog reported after two too many wines one night). 'We should give her a two-syllable name,' he had added, before passing out on his second celebratory joint. Mog, awash with hormones, had obligingly called the fledgling 'O-live'. Unfortunately, Mog had packed her bags a fortnight later when WilliamPetersMustardSeed shacked up with another woman, leaving Olive, Mog and their two-by-one family.

But even with a perfectly symmetrical family, body and bedroom, there was always something absent with Olive – she had only ever felt half. She didn't feel half from her waist down or from her waist up; it was more abstract than that. 'Is the glass half full or half empty?' Mog always asked. Half full/half empty was Mog's test for whether a person was a pessimist or an optimist.

Mog was a half-full, sunny type of woman, even though the house was messy and she'd had to become a barrister because life hadn't dealt her the hand she'd expected. But to Olive it didn't really matter: half full or half empty, there was still a lot missing.

What happened to Olive, however, wasn't because she'd only ever felt half. It didn't even happen because her house was full of knick-knacks and clutter, because she called her mother Mog, or because she knew of a man named WilliamPetersMustardSeed. It wasn't because she had a peculiar relationship with the number two, or because her skin was the exact colour of chicken loaf. Although there was never any doubt that it was a shake-it-all-about hokey-pokey of all these things, what happened to Olive couldn't have happened without Mathilda Graham.

2
Pleasing Mathilda

It was Friday afternoon at the Joanne d'Arc School for Girls. Olive stood waiting for Mathilda at the gates as the grounds thinned.

Mathilda finally emerged, a freshly brushed ponytail frizzing behind her. She looked Olive up and then down. Her gaze narrowed at Olive's feet. 'Why do you always stand like that? It makes you waddle – like a duck.' Olive blushed and shuffled her toes back in together. Recently, Mathilda had started walking with a very slight pigeon toe. Olive vowed to affect a pigeon toe herself.

Olive picked up her school bag and she and Mathilda set off towards the crossing.

'Hey – Olive! Mathilda! Stable-West said to give these to you.'

Lim May Yee came puffing up behind the girls, holding out two envelopes.

Olive didn't know Lim May Yee very well. She was a boarder and tended to stick to her kind. Lim May Yee's name was a source of great confusion in the school. She insisted on having 'Lim May Yee' on the roll but she wrote 'May Lim' on her homework. Was she Lim? Was she May? What was with the Yee? The teachers, not knowing what to call her, settled for the whole kit 'n' caboodle, Lim May Yee, just to be on the safe side. The boarders called her Pud.

Lim May Yee smiled. 'They're just tickets for the Christmas concert – for your parents.' She gave a short wave and ran off ahead to catch up with a group of boarders who were already across the crossing and halfway down the hill to the milk bar.

Mathilda's envelope bulged. She opened it – despite the fact it was addressed to her mother – and sighed. 'I had to get six tickets even though the maximum was actually four.'

'Oh,' said Olive. She clutched her envelope with its single ticket inside. Tickets and notices were always for paren*ts* and never for paren*t*. People assumed. Even if a girl's parents were divorced, they assumed she had two – maybe even three or four – stuffed in different homes. Asking after a paren*t* was as abnormal as asking somebody whether they wore bed soc*k* or ate pe*a*.

Mathilda zipped her fat wad of tickets into her school bag and the girls stepped onto the crossing. 'Do you mind if I stay?'

'Of course not.' Olive grinned and her tummy soared. Mathilda liked aspects of Olive's house. Mog had arranged accounts at the newsagent's and the chemist and Olive was allowed to put whatever she wanted on them. Mathilda thought that was marvellous. Mathilda also thought Mog's nail polish collection was marvellous, and the girls had spent most of Grade 6 painting each nail on their hands and toes a different shade of red. For French cosmetics and air-freighted magazines, Mathilda was willing to put up with any amount of chaos and clutter.

'Can we catch a taxi home?'

'Sure,' said Olive, who usually did.

'Here,' said Mathilda. 'Pass me your phone. I'll call.'

Olive had her own mobile with her own plan. Mathilda wasn't even allowed pre-paid, but Olive always let her text, whenever she wanted.

Olive excavated the phone from her bag. Mathilda punched a few buttons and it burst into song. 'What's that ringtone?' Mathilda scrunched her nose and stuffed the phone up her sleeve to dull the metallic chirping. She looked over both shoulders.

'It's a virus and I don't know how to get rid of it.' Olive blushed again. This was not actually true. Olive knew exactly how to get rid of it, because she'd put it on; it was Johanna's bird song from the musical *Sweeney Todd*.

Olive loved musicals. Sometimes, when Mog had the night off, they would sit through double features at an old cinema with cracked leather seats, watching *Singin' in the Rain*, *Funny Girl* and *Cabaret*. On the way home, Mog and Olive would swing their arms, click their heels, and bellow out all the words. Those movies made Olive tinkle; they made her feel like she could fly.

'Hmm, I just love Fridays,' said Mathilda once the chirping had stopped and she'd called a taxi. She popped Olive's phone in her bag.

'Why?' asked Olive, deeply relieved that the subject of the ringtone had been abandoned (even if her phone had been appropriated in the process).

'Olive. Der! Because there's such a stretch until school again.' Mathilda studied her shoes while they walked, obviously irritated that her mother had once again polished over the carefully cultivated scuff marks.

'Oh, me too. Love Fridays,' said Olive, but she didn't sound very convincing. Olive studied her own T-bars, which shone in the afternoon light. As she walked, she tried to keep her feet at least parallel to the kerb.

It was strange, but Olive had never actually thought about enjoying weekends. Unless she was hanging out with Mathilda, she usually just sat around waiting for class again, waiting to chat. Sometimes Olive was so bored that she became completely inert: arms leaden and lips thick. On those days (usually Sundays), Olive felt too heavy to move from the couch; she couldn't even pick up her paints. She'd just sit there, listening to the hum of the beach market down the street, as blank as the pages of the watercolour pad on her lap.

Mathilda's house, on the other hand, was always teeming with kids, and swimsuits hung out to dry on the line in rows, and bundled trainers that smelled of salt water and rubber. The cupboards were filled with scratched hand-me-down hockey sticks, and violins, and bent white mouthguards with bits of somebody else's Shreddies in them, which Olive did find a bit disgusting. But there was always somebody to play Monopoly with; Scrabble with; to hit (or miss) a ball with. Even though Mathilda whinged about not having any sisters, Olive thought her incredibly lucky.

Olive looked up. Amelia Forster was sitting on the fence of a nearby house, waiting for her mum with a tennis racket and a tan. Amelia looked like a piece of sun-kissed caramel – sun-kissed caramel with a ski-jump nose and sparkling smile.

Amelia Forster was the most desired girl in Year 7: class captain in first term every year since Prep; netball captain; Mary in the upcoming Christmas concert – the *Centennial* Christmas Concert. She had effortless style, pretty pretty eyes, pierced ears and a holiday house with a tennis court. She also stood and walked with a very slight pigeon toe, which had gained a cult following in Year 7 as a result.

'That is so true.'

'What is?' Olive looked at Mathilda, who was back on the mobile. Olive didn't recall it ringing. 'Who are you . . . ?'

Mathilda threw Olive a *not-now* look. She shook her noodle curls (brushing them out never lasted long) and laughed. 'Hmmm,' she said coyly. Then, after a quick pause, 'Hmmm' again. The girls were now level with Amelia Forster's trainers.

Mathilda flicked Amelia a smile and gestured at the phone in a *you understand this is a crucial social moment* sort of way.

Olive went to smile at Amelia too, but Amelia had dipped into her school bag; Olive just smiled at the space where Amelia's pout had hung.

The girls turned down a side street to meet their taxi.

'See ya,' said Mathilda and put the phone back in her bag.

'Who was that?' asked Olive, wondering who was so wise and how they knew her number.

'Just a friend. *Ouch!*' Mathilda gave her shoulder an exaggerated rub and stepped away from Olive.

'Sorry,' said Olive, whose arms swung a bit too irreverently when she walked. It was hard to concentrate on holding a heavy bag, walking with a pigeon toe and avoiding the cracks.

'Well, you should watch where you're going, Ol. You always bump into me and it kills.'

Olive stared out of the window as the taxi driver drove the girls home. While Mrs Graham said that Olive lived out in the sticks, the description wasn't strictly accurate. For Mrs Graham, any trip that involved longer than seven minutes in the car may as well have been to the country, and in fact, the suburb in which the Grahams lived (and the girls went to school) was a lot stickier – well, greener anyway. It had nature strips of emerald grass thick enough to roll in – although nobody ever did – and roundabouts that toasted spring with flowers (English, colour-themed) and winter with herbs (French). The roads wrapped around parks where well-pressed children played cricket and collected their dogs'

grammed bags. The homes, tucked behind
dges, were all different, unique, yet they fitted
ike a string of freshwater pearls.

n where Olive and Mog lived, the streets were
loose — as bleached and broad as airport runways. They
were lined up next to each other in rows and led to the
beach, which lay like a discarded towel, bumpy and
bitten, at their feet. The buildings were thrown together,
mismatched and chipped, like shelves of charity shop
crockery. Some houses had turrets, others balconies with
pillars as curly as candy canes. A couple were stumpy
and thickset. Olive's house stood tall and red – the only
red-brick home in a suburb of peeling paint.

'She sticks out like a true redhead,' Mog said. Olive
didn't see how that was a good thing: most red-nuts at
school had no friends.

The neighbours didn't water their gardens. They
didn't say hi. The whole suburb was bathed in sweat and
salt and lit with the neon-blue of laundrettes. While it
was sometimes cooler than the collared suburbs, the
evening breeze was rank with seaweed.

When they got home, Mathilda poked around the
garden while Olive fumbled about in her school bag for
the key. It was a rule: the quicker Olive tried to find anything, the slower she was.

'What is that anyway?' Mathilda called. She was looking at a tiny shed dug deep into the corner of the garden
and covered with ivy.

'The bomb shelter,' said Olive, joining her. The bomb
shelter was a squat damp room with no windows.

Mathilda rattled the doorknob. 'What's it for?'

'Mog said it was built in case the Japanese came to Australia during World War Two.'

'To lock them in?' Mathilda assumed the look she used for maths – a calculated blend of irritation, confusion and disinterest.

'I guess so,' said Olive even though she knew that was absolutely not the case.

'That's dumb. I can't imagine why anyone would want to lock them in.' Mathilda shook her ponytail and poked her head inside. Olive cringed; she'd assumed the shelter would be locked.

'Um, maybe it was to lock us in,' said Olive tentatively, picking over her words, hoping to distract Mathilda from the mess. 'To protect us from them?'

Mathilda turned pink and slammed the door. 'Gross. It's so full of crap they'd never fit anyway.'

Olive turned her back to Mathilda, hand trembling with the key. She knew Mathilda was right, and she felt deeply ashamed. Behind her, the red bricks of the bomb shelter blushed in sympathy.

Once Olive finally managed to open the back door, Mathilda walked in and headed straight to the pantry.

'Sorry, but there's nothing,' said Olive, following. 'I haven't shopped.'

Mathilda opened the pantry door, sweeping Olive out of the way. Mathilda loved processed food and often snuck money from her mum's handbag to buy lollies. Unfortunately, however, Olive was right: apart from pasta shells, soy sauce and capers, the cupboard was

15

empty. Mathilda looked every bit as put out as she obviously felt.

'Let's go to Babette's Feast,' suggested Olive. 'We can take Mog's Visa card.'

Mog always left a Visa debit card tucked in an envelope on the fridge for emergencies (fire/flood/famine). This, Olive felt, qualified as famine.

'Cool.' Mathilda looked perkier. 'Can we dress up?'

Olive shrugged. 'If you want.' Mog was very relaxed about things like that. Mrs Graham didn't let the girls into her wardrobe, although she had once shown them her wedding gown and Olive had never forgotten. It was a dress made from thick ivory velvet, which was soft and heartbreakingly beautiful. It had tiny antique buttons that shimmered in a line, all the way from the nape of the neck to the floor. Olive had sunk her fingers into the creamy fabric and shivered as she swept them along it. It was the first time she had really wished that Mog had married too.

Mathilda rummaged through the drawers in Mog's dressing room, fingering silky stockings and lacy petticoats, which smelled like lily-of-the-valley. 'Mog really does have the best clothes. If I lived here, I'd never be out of them.' She pulled on a skirt and a pair of high-heeled shoes with diamanté clasps at the ankle; she wound chiffon and silk scarves around her neck, and a thick belt around her hips. Mathilda wanted to be a fashion designer when she grew up, with shops in Paddington and Paris, and a range of scented candles to earn proper money.

16

Olive flicked through the racks. 'Mog's always on the hunt for "jaw-dropping" frocks. She likes beautiful things.' *And not so beautiful things*, she thought, tucking a bracelet made from a knitting needle into the top drawer.

Mathilda shuffled off to study the photos on Mog's mantelpiece. 'Is this your dad?'

Olive didn't discuss her father with anyone, not even Mathilda, although she did often think about him. All Olive knew was that he and Mog had split when she was born, and that Mog had had 'zip' to do with him since. Olive's father was christened William Peters but he'd changed his name by deed poll to Mustard Seed, because he liked mustard and because he was what Mog called a 'flaky hippy'. WilliamPetersMustardSeed was too free with his love for Mog.

Mathilda was examining a new photo Olive's Uncle John had sent. 'Nope. That's my uncle,' said Olive.

The kids at school sometimes teased Olive and said that Mog was a lesbian because she hadn't found a man since WilliamPetersMustardSeed. But if Mog was a lesbian, she wasn't a very good one. She never brought anybody home.

'Uncle John's a doctor. He works with kids in Nigeria.'

'Oh,' said Mathilda, in a voice that meant she didn't care about Uncle John, and that Mog must be a lesbian after all.

Unlike Mog, Mathilda's mum was a proper mum. She was brusque and organized and ran the Graham family like the army.

'Come on, troops!' she'd cry. '*En avant*. Let's keep the chaos to a minimum.'

She baked her own cakes and stewed her own marmalade and she ran the school fête and ferried all the Graham children between soccer trials and choir practice and gymnastics and Chinese lessons and découpage and flute. She sewed sequins onto trainers and wind-cheaters that she sold from the back of her people carrier to raise money for the school's new sports centre. She wrote hundreds of lists with tick-boxes, which she left for her 'brood' (Mrs Graham called her kids her 'brood') in helpful places.

☐ Have you got your sunscreen?
☐ Your hat?
☐ Your gym gear?

Olive thought she was wonderful. Mathilda, however, would have traded any amount of homemade cake and marmalade for a Visa card and freedom.

Mathilda had started reading Mog's Christmas cards. Olive straightened them and put the one Mathilda was holding back on the shelf. 'I'm starving. Let's get something to eat.'

'Great,' said Mathilda, whose thirst for gossip was trumped only by her thirst for junk food. She tugged at her top, which had ridden up over the doughnut of flesh around her middle, wiped away a smear of eyeliner, and thrust out her bosoms. 'You got the plastic?'

Olive held up her wallet.

Mathilda puffed her curls and spun away from the mirror. Her grin cut from one ear to the other. 'C'mon, Olive Garnaut, let's blow this joint.'

3

Pressed Lips and Proper Mums

Olive and Mathilda hobbled down to Babette's Feast with pigeon toes and too-big lipsticked mouths. Olive ordered blueberry smoothies and slabs of caramel slice.

'Don't you want a main meal?' asked the waiter. 'I can recommend the pesto linguini.'

Olive looked at Mathilda.

'Perhaps some garlic bread,' said Mathilda. 'Two portions.'

The waiter sniffed and his nostrils pinched together. Mathilda and Olive laughed bubbles into their blueberry smoothies.

'Let's hop on the swings,' yelled Mathilda after the café. She ran off towards the kids' playground on the foreshore, scarves trailing.

Mathilda and Olive swung high, trying to lance the sun with their heels before it sank into the horizon. Olive watched as the sky turned pink and then inky.

'Do you want to get an ice cream? From Okey Doke's?' Summer or winter, Olive ate ice cream until her head ached and her lips turned purple. Okey Doke's stall stood in the beach car park, battered by the wind and a strong current of loyal patrons. The shop was actually called Tackle Togs 'n' Takeaway, but Olive called the owner Okey Doke because whenever she ordered ice cream he responded, 'Okey doke, artichoke,' every time. Olive would then monitor him carefully while he smeared the confectionery onto the cone, in case he slipped in a suspect flavour – a flavour just like artichoke. He never did.

Mathilda shook her head. 'Nah.' She had wandered over to some women who were twirling flaming batons. The women were dancing and spinning, their full stomachs greased and yellow in the light.

Olive sat on a bluestone wall watching the dancers until she was distracted by a family with a gaggle of kids playing together. They were just like the Grahams, that family, she thought. As she stared, Olive tried to work out which kid looked like which parent. The kids were bickering.

'Give it here, yer loser. Muuuuarrm, Braedon's got my frisbee and 'e won't giveitback.'

Olive wondered how they could fight when they were so lucky to have that many kids living out in the sticks with them. The father of the kid called Braedon ran into the middle of the mob and held the frisbee above his head, hopping from one foot to the other to keep it from the kids while they pawed at his shirt. Olive looked away.

Olive always told herself she didn't need a father, but when she saw one her yearning came barrelling back and the ache was real.

This yearning was private, anonymous; it had no name. Girls at school yearned for music and new skirts and tarts they could cook in the toaster. There wasn't anything bad about these desires, but Olive thought them rice-cracker wishes, insubstantial.

Sometimes Olive tugged out her eyelashes. She pulled them out in little clumps, and the sting distracted her from her wanting for a moment. Olive collected the eyelashes, as fine and pale as they were, and wished on them, but she couldn't wish for a father on an eyelash: a father wouldn't fit. A father wouldn't fit on a birthday candle, or on the surface of coins thrown into the park fountain, either. A wish like a father was too cumbersome, too heavy.

Mog had once taken Olive to see Father Christmas on a forty-degree day. 'Now, what would you like this year?' he had asked with brandied cheer as Olive sat on his knee. Olive had let her sandal-heavy feet dangle. Cupped in Father Christmas's thick lap, she felt she'd finally found a place big enough for her wish.

That Christmas, Olive had woken to a bicycle.

The kids' father put the frisbee in his bag. 'We'd better head off,' he said. 'It's getting dark.'

Olive looked around for Mathilda. The father was right. Mog wouldn't like them hanging around in the park after dark, either. Olive stood and walked back towards her friend. Mathilda wasn't watching the dancers any more. She was sitting on the bluestone fence that divided the park from the beach, curling a ringlet around her finger. She was staring at two baggy boys gnawing hamburgers on the sand. They were staring back.

'Hey,' said Olive. 'What are you up to?'

The baggy boys turned with their burgers to the sea.

Mathilda glanced from Olive to the boys and back again. Then she leaned down and undid a diamanté clasp. 'My feet are killing,' she said. 'Let's go.'

When they got home, Olive ran a huge bubble bath. Mog had a bath with feet, which stood with splayed toes in the middle of her bathroom. The tips of its claws had chipped polish where Olive had once varnished them in Ruby Woo.

Olive always sat at the deep end of the bath. She had convinced herself years ago that if she didn't sit in the deep end, she'd contract some horrible disease and would have to spend the rest of her life in pain and dire poverty. Once a girl had made a rule like that, it was hard to fly in the face of it. Although Mathilda didn't actually know this, she always let Olive sit in the deep end because that was the end with the plug (which she said hurt her bottom).

While they were in the bath, the telephone rang. 'Bags not getting it,' said Mathilda and Olive at exactly the same time. The water had cooled to the point where it was too cold to stay in and too cold to get out. As the phone rang on, the girls huddled under the greasy water and bickered happily over who would (not) tend to the call until it stopped. Then started again.

'Oh, I will.' Olive clutched the enamel sides of the bath.

'Don't worry about it. It'll just be my mum. I forgot to tell her I was coming – I'll ring when we get out.' Mathilda turned on the hot-water tap, which spat hot drips.

'Whoops,' screeched Olive, 'we've drained the tank. Again!'

'I'm freezing.' Mathilda stood up and grabbed Mog's towel.

'What do you want to do next?' asked Olive, shivering in the tepid water.

'Internet?' Mathilda loved chat rooms. She wasn't allowed into them at home, but Mog didn't have any issues with them.

'Chat rooms? What a lovely invention,' Mog had once said. She thought that crime stayed in her chambers. 'In my day, we had pen friends.'

Olive took the damp towel and changed as quickly and discreetly as possible. When she emerged from the bathroom, Mathilda was back reading Mog's Christmas cards, draining the last of Olive's Coke straight from the bottle.

'I'll meet you in the study.' Olive passed the light switch and thought, just for one moment, about switching it off.

'Move over.' Mathilda took up the driving seat behind

the keyboard. 'You're such a hog. You always take the best seat.'

'Sorry,' said Olive. 'I was just turning the monitor on.'

Mathilda crossed one leg. She was wearing Mog's bathrobe and had knotted her hair on top of her head. She typed in an address. 'This one's great,' she said as the web page flashed onto the screen. 'Real desperados.'

A bloke called Sinus was online.

Hi Sinus, this is Salami, typed Mathilda.
How big's ur salami? Sinus typed straight back.
Hot.
But how big?
Bigger than urs ;) wrote Mathilda.

Even though the room was empty, Olive looked over her shoulder. 'Do you think we should do this?'

'You're such a worrywart, Olive. It's cheeky. I happen to be very good at sexual innuendo because of my three brothers. Dad says they speak nothing but sexual innuendo.'

Olive laughed, but only a bit. She didn't exactly know what sexual innuendo was. 'But what if Sinus can track us?'

'Just don't wor-' Mathilda was interrupted by the doorbell.

Olive walked down the hall to find Mrs Graham red-faced and blustery on the veranda. A few black noodle curls had escaped from her combs and stuck to her doughy face.

'Hello, Olive. Is Mathilda here?' Mrs Graham looked

Olive up and down. Olive smelled like grape bubble bath, and she was scratching a rash that had sprung up behind her knee. Olive stopped scratching as Mrs Graham's lips tightened.

Mathilda moseyed down to see who was at the door. Despite the bath, her face was streaked with ruined make-up. Her tongue was cola-brown.

'I have been trying to get through on the phone for hours, Mathilda.' Mrs Graham's voice was as tight as her pink-frosted lips.

'Oh, sorry, Mrs Graham,' said Olive. 'We've been on the Internet and we don't have broadband yet.'

Mathilda didn't say anything. She just rubbed her mouth along Mog's bathrobe sleeve.

Olive invited Mrs Graham inside. Mrs Graham gave her a clipped nod and strode straight down the hall. 'Collect your belongings, Mathilda. *Pronto.*'

Olive knew Mrs Graham always used the word pronto when she was cross. Because it was Spanish, she rolled the 'r': p*rrrrrr*onto. Olive watched as Mrs Graham walked into Mog's study, ahead of the girls. She looked up at the walls, which had yellowed with smoke and age, and pushed her tight lips tighter. *You could press flowers between those lips*, thought Olive. *They'd be as effective as phone books*.

Before either Olive or Mathilda could protest, Mrs Graham walked over to the computer and read the exchange between Salami and Sinus. Later, according to Mathilda, Mrs Graham would tell Mr Graham that the girls had been engaging perverts who could have lured them with promises of meetings with That Paris Hilton. For the time being, however, she asked one question: 'Where is your mother, Olive?' And when Olive couldn't deliver the right response, Mrs Graham and her pressed lips drove Mathilda home. Without another word.

4
Metal-detecting

Ten days later, the sky sagged and the rain set in. Olive was stuck watching water trickle down the windows and the insides of the walls. Mog had forgotten to call the man to fix the roof tiles *again*.

Olive was in a mood, and she was bored – bored in the sort of way a kid can only be if she's made to sit through four hours of Wagnerian opera or to hang about watching the rain after school without her best friend. Mathilda wasn't at Olive's because she wasn't allowed to come over any more. While Olive was *more than welcome* to stay at Mathilda's, where the Grahams could *keep an eye on them*, Olive didn't want to.

Olive had gone to Mathilda's once or twice since The Incident, but she'd felt the Grahams' simultaneous sympathy and disapproval with each visit. As Olive had sat in their kitchen tearing date scones from buttery trays and watching Mathilda swat her brothers with a tea towel, she had felt like a traitor; a traitor deserting Mog, their weekends in junk stores, her jaw-dropping frocks and every single one of their dust-covered knick-knacks.

While Olive waited for Mog to get home, she tried to find things to do. She waded through junk to the computer in Mog's study, where she logged on to the chat room she and Mathilda had mucked about on. Olive read all the entries, but Sinus wasn't there – there were just two kids called Spanakopita and Ironic talking about character development in *Harry Potter and the Goblet of Fire*. Olive abandoned them and found a search engine instead.

Olive loved search engines and often ran Google searches, spelling 'Mustard Seed and William Peters' carefully, although she never found anything. Tonight was no different. Olive did a search for 'Mog Garnaut' and scrolled through the files. She studied the photos of her mother, who looked sterner and older under her grey Bo Peep work wig. Olive noted which web pages were new and printed them out for her diary. She liked to keep track of Mog like that; it made Mog feel closer.

When Olive had finished, she switched off the computer. The house fell poison-still.

Maybe I should just catch a taxi to Mathilda's after all, she thought. Maybe the Grahams didn't *really* disapprove of her. It could be lovely. She could watch Mr Graham while he did suitable dad-like things, such as putting up picture hooks, carving the roast lamb and helping himself to chutney. Then she and Mathilda could sit in the drawing room while Mr Graham read to them from *His Dark Materials*. The curtains in the drawing room had aqua checks *in chintz* to match the aqua-checked poof and the shiny aqua door on the cover of the book on the coffee table.

Before Olive could indulge in too many more Graham-family domestic fantasies, a fat drop of water hit her on the nose. 'No!' she cried. Water had migrated from the walls to the middle of the ceiling. Leaks had also spouted in the hall, and everything was getting wet.

Olive spent the next hour darting through towers of junk, strategically placing pots, pans and towels on the carpet. While she was plonking a particularly large saucepan under a particularly virile leak in the billiard room, a big brown box tumbled down from a stack of junk. She ducked. A blue-green metallic contraption rolled out onto the floorboards, where it lay gleaming like a new bike. It had a long handle and a flat disc at the base that was connected to a number of levers and wires. Olive was still trying to work out what it was when Mog walked in.

'What a day, what a day.' Mog kissed Olive on her forehead just where it met the tip of her parting. It was 9.45 p.m. and neither of them had eaten. 'I thought you said Mathilda was coming over?'

'She just left,' Olive lied. Mog hated it when Olive was alone. She always seemed much happier knowing that Olive was hanging out with other girls – as if it was a way to gauge if Olive was normal or something. Besides, Mog would be furious if she knew the real reason Mathilda hadn't been there. Olive fetched two bowls and the muesli.

'Oh dear,' said Mog. 'It's hardly meat and three veg. Try not to pick out the raisins.'

Olive sat with a placemat at the table, methodically picking out the raisins. Mog ate standing at the fridge, whizzing through the post and listening to phone messages.

'That council,' said Mog. 'Now they're putting electronic chips in dogs to track them – injecting them square into their rumps. Barbaric carcinogens. What's this country coming to?' She sighed in a *hmph* through her nose and went back to the post.

'And that school of yours,' she continued, shredding a glossy update. 'I'd just like to know when students became "clients" and parents "stakeholders"? If I'd wanted to have you schooled in a corporation, I'd at least have picked a listed company.' As Mog spoke, she threw up her hands to *Prove! The! Point!* like an exclamation mark of elbows and wrists before dumping the post in the recycling pile. If she noticed the saucepans filling with water, the soggy towels or the leaky roof, she didn't say anything, and Olive didn't draw her attention to them.

After dinner, Olive put the muesli bowls in the dishwasher and continued to fiddle with the contraption.

'What have you got that old thing for?' Mog was standing over Olive with the home phone clutched to her ear. Olive shrugged.

'It's an old metal detector I picked up somewhere yonks ago,' said Mog. 'Oh, I think we might have needed it for a play. But you know what they say: something lost is something found.' She laughed. 'That saying certainly made me feel better whenever I lost things – my bag, my mascara, you at the drycleaner . . . bugger.' Mog's mobile was ringing. With the home phone clamped between her head and a shoulder, she picked up her mobile and went to fend off another crisis.

Olive found the owner's manual for the metal detector in the bottom of the box. It showed a man in a soft hat drawing a grid on the sand. His face had a studied, inquisitive look that made him look like George Bush or the village idiot, but Olive would draw a grid too. It was good to be thorough. With a grid, she would be sure to avoid covering the same patch of beach twice.

In her mind, Olive could see herself walking patiently backwards and forwards. She could hear the bleep of the metal detector as it thrust its nose into the sand, and she could see the headlines plastered across every newsstand already:

TWELVE-YEAR-OLD GIRL UNEARTHS LONG-LOST *TITANIC*
BULLION ON LOCAL BEACH

Bullion was a fancy word for treasure. This metal detector was going to be the most exciting thing that had ever happened to Olive Garnaut.

She just knew it.

5
Ditched

The next afternoon, Olive walked home with lucky-coin ice cream on her breath and the metal detector in her hand. She hadn't found lost *Titanic* bullion, or even Roman coins, but she had found two dollars, which she'd put straight towards an ice cream. She'd watched the coin as it dropped into Okey Doke's tubby hand. It was lovely to think that a lucky coin like that would now be in circulation. *Man, wait until Mathilda hears about this*, thought Olive. The potential was endless.

'Watch it!'

'Whoops, sorry.' Olive was so distracted, she'd walked into a man with a fisherman's cap. The metal detector had hit him square in the stomach. The man with the fisherman's cap looked at the contraption and his face softened. 'A metal detector. Golly, I haven't seen one of those for a while. You find anything?'

'A tin of boot polish, some rusty fishhooks and two dollars.'

'Not bad. Stick at it – you could find more.'

'Like what?'

'Oh, keys to a mansion, pirate treasure, the Honourable Harold Holt. That sort of thing.'

Olive looked blank.

'The former Prime Minister who disappeared in Mysterious Circumstances further along the coast.' The man smiled, and the white stubble on his chin rippled.

'Do you really think so?' Olive looked down at the man's dog. Mog said she didn't trust men with small dogs, but this one was a little West Highland terrier. 'A Westie!' she said. 'My best friend, Mathilda, has one of those. Mathilda Graham – she's my best friend. What's your dog's name?'

'Jones,' said the man in the fisherman's cap.

'Mathilda's is called Cassie. I actually can't wait to tell Mathilda about this metal detector, even if I haven't got much yet. I kept it a secret today, because I wanted to see whether it actually works. Now I know it does, we'll have a go together after school tomorrow. If she's allowed. Mathilda might have a bit more luck than me – she tends to.' The words tumbled out before Olive could catch them.

'You always such a chatterbox?' The man in the fisherman's cap laughed.

'No,' said Olive, and the truth was that she wasn't. Olive Garnaut was quiet, really; she always had been.

❋ ❋ ❋

By the time Olive got home, the moon sat low and lumpy in the sky. Olive held her key out in front of her as she made her way to the back door. She tried not to look at the tree shadows that plucked worms from the garden and moths from the sky with their long twiggy fingers. She plunged towards the lock and stumbled, then scuttled inside and bolted the door.

Even indoors, however, Olive couldn't relax. She stomped into each room, turning on lights; colonizing the unknown with each flick of the switch. Only after this was done could Olive breathe.

When the house was blazing and her heart had steadied, Olive checked the answering machine. The light was flashing. Olive loved the old answering machine; she particularly loved it when it flashed. *Hello*, it seemed to say. *Thinking of you. Remember that you are somebody.*

There was only one message and it was from Mog.

'Hi, Ol. Hope you had a lovely day. Bad news. Just realized that I've gone and accepted dinner with the Attorney-General on the night of your concert. It is a slippery year – Christmas already. I hope you don't mind, darling. I know it's not ideal, but it's the only day he's in town before he heads off for his summer break. I thought you could come along after the concert. We can ask Mathilda, too. I'll call later to discuss. Love Mog.'

Mog always signed off her answering-machine messages like they were emails or letters she was dictating. Olive hated it. She kicked at a pile of papers. How could Mog go and do that? *Slippery year, my foot.* The

Christmas concert was sacred. It was the one evening when Mog was there with the other girls' parents, *guaranteed*. Afterwards they'd have burnt urn coffee in the foyer with the teachers, and Olive would lean against Mog and feel like them. This year was even more important, because Olive's art might be chosen for display. Olive kicked out at the papers again.

It actually wasn't unusual for Mog and Olive to dine with politicians like the Attorney-General. In fact, they often had dinner with politicians and their families on Sunday nights, for what Mog called 'relaxed quality family time' – but they never ate in. Instead, they went to suitably casual-for-the-kids bistros, where Olive could order spaghetti with meat sauce and lick the bolognese off each strand.

Sometimes Olive fell asleep at the table, and when she woke she'd have bits of meat sauce in her hair. 'I'd better be getting this one to bed,' Mog would say. But she would always have another glass of red wine – 'for the road' – and Olive rarely remembered the taxi ride home.

And that was to be Olive's first senior-school concert? Her art – maybe the only Year 7 art – could be on display, and while all the other parents studied it, her mother would be studying a politician who blow-dried his hair?

Olive picked up the phone. Mathilda would understand. Even though Mrs Graham had never missed a single concert, and in fact served the biscuits, Mathilda would get it.

It took some time for Mathilda to answer. 'Hi, Ol, I've got to be quick. The boys have their school Christmas barbecue picnic tonight and Mum's making us all go.'

Olive had heard other girls talking about the Christmas barbecue picnic earlier in the day. As much as Mathilda moaned, it sounded quite fun. Apparently everyone sat on blankets and held candles, in cups to stop the drips running down their hands, while they ate crackers and cold chicken.

'That's OK,' said Olive, wishing she had a brother, too. Olive paused, hoping Mathilda might include her.

Mathilda didn't. 'Guess what? I'm getting a lift with Amelia – in her dad's convertible!'

Amelia Forster's father wore cufflinks and drove a car with the numberplate VAT (no numbers). He had made his fortune in tax. 'Crass,' both Mog and Mrs Graham had agreed in a rare moment, although the girls had thought that it would be rather delicious to drive with windy hair.

'Oh,' said Olive. 'Say hi to Amelia.' She said goodbye and hung up.

Olive walked to the bathroom, mouth and limbs saggy. Shadows skulked behind the boxes in the hall. Baths were a good cure-all, Mog said – baths and hot-water bottles. And they both were.

Olive waited until the tub had filled before she undressed, breathing in the steam. As she climbed in, the water rose reassuringly up the bath's sides. Olive had matter. She did matter. The water folded around her limbs and held her.

Once Olive was warm in her pyjamas, she made some Vegemite toast. She buttered it quickly and evenly so that the butter and the Vegemite would melt in together before the toast got cold. Olive took the plate and a glass of water and fell back into the couch with Mog's old photo album.

Mog had been a hippy when she was a student. Now having a hippy past just meant that Mog felt guilty when she accepted plastic bags, and that they'd get takeaway Thai rather than McDonald's. But the album featured shots of Mog when she was young – all hairy armpitted and nut brown. Looking at the photos, Olive could imagine WilliamPetersMustardSeed holding Olive while bongo drums beat; both brown as berries and swinging free.

Olive liked to examine the photos for signs of Him. *I bet he wouldn't miss a Centennial Christmas Concert with an art show for the Attorney-General*. She studied the photos. Did the thigh towering behind her mother (in the yoga lotus pose) belong to him? Were they his dark glasses on the coffee table? Was that his Joni Mitchell T-shirt, taut over Mog's swollen tummy? Olive shook her toast over the page. If WilliamPetersMustardSeed was there, a crumb would land on him to prove it.

The toast crumbs were picked up in a draught that shot through the house. Olive sighed. The answer was blowing in the wind.

Olive's dreamings were interrupted by the phone. It was Mog's new secretary, Trudy, who spoke in squawks like a cockatoo. 'Hi, Olive. Your mum's been trying to get through to you. I'll pop her on.'

Mog gushed onto the phone. 'Hi, darling! How are

you? How was your day? How's Mathilda? Did you hand in your Ming dynasty assignment?'

Mog always did this. She shot off a series of questions, leaving no room for the answers. But Mog always remembered one thing that Olive had on each day, and she always asked about it. Although Olive was cross, she liked the fact Mog tried.

'Fine thanks,' said Olive neatly. 'I didn't get much down at the beach with the metal detector, but I'm going to try again tomorrow. When will you be home?'

Olive tried to hide the whinge in her voice. Mog hated whingers, but Olive could feel it creeping up her throat. She took a big gulp of water to push the whinge back down.

'I'm sorry, Ol. You know I'm stuck on a Big Case.'

'But it's been two years.'

There was a silence. 'Ol, it hasn't been quite that long. Anyway, I should be home shortly. Tuck yourself into bed with a hottie and I'll turn out the lights when I get in.'

'OK.'

'And about the concert, darling. I'm sorry about it – *really* sorry about it. I owe you one. Big time. Oh, and stick to the back of the beach. I always lose stuff in the soft sand at the back. We'll have a shot on the weekend if you like. Client's waiting. Better go. Love you!'

The line clicked and went blank. The thing was, thought Olive, Mog really would feel sorry about it, desperately sorry. She always did. But Mog was frightfully ambitious. 'She nurtures that media profile more than her daughter,' Olive had overheard a tennis-and-tuckshop mum whisper once. The other mums had all murmured their agreement. Most of the time, Olive didn't care what they thought. In fact, most of the time she was actually proud.

Mog, like Olive, was very skinny, with the same hair, only Mog's was cut in a professional bob and had darkened to honey with age. Mog wore lipstick and high-heeled shoes and the press always mentioned her lovely long pins. Mog said that this was 'ridiculous' and 'offensive', and that it had absolutely nothing to do with her performance on behalf of her clients – which was, she noted, always 'sterling'. Olive noticed, however, that Mog continued to wear sliced skirts (which did show off her rather nice legs).

Olive often wondered if the tennis-and-tuckshop mums and WilliamPetersMustardSeed watched Mog on the evening news when she did.

Mog was ambitious because she wanted to be a judge. At the moment she was a QC, or Queen's Counsel, which Mog said just meant she was darn good at her job and a super role model for young women. It was weird though, thought Olive, because Australia didn't have a queen, only Crown Princess Mary, who would be the Queen of Denmark, not Australia.

When Mog wasn't working she spent the evenings hobnobbing with politicians – like the Attorney-General – because politicians appointed Queen's Counsel as judges. As far as Olive knew, Crown Princess Mary didn't appoint judges. Which might explain why Mog had never invited Mary to dinner.

Olive closed the album. Even with all that royal waving to do, Olive was sure Crown Princess Mary would be in the front row at her kids' concerts. As Olive headed for bed, she kicked out at a random tower of Mog's trinkets in the hall. They scattered and shattered. Olive left them where they fell.

6
Then Dumped

The next morning at school, conversation was dominated by tales of the Christmas barbecue picnic. Mathilda told everyone how her family and Amelia Forster's family had sat on rugs next to each other. The girls had snuggled in under a blanket while Mr Graham pointed out crosses and saucepans and pink planets in the sky.

Olive had stared at the stars one night herself with Mr Graham, trying to find those exact constellations. Olive had pretended as best she could, but she'd had no idea what Mr Graham was talking about. They'd just looked like stars.

This was not, however, Amelia Forster's experience. 'It was brilliant,' she boasted. 'We also saw Jupiter, and we're going to use it to tell our own horoscopes.'

That would be right, thought Olive. Amelia was so talented she could probably even see the African animals in those fuzzy drawings that merged if you looked at them in the right way.

Amelia and Mathilda talked about the picnic all the way through English and into Art. Olive tried to change the topic. She wanted to discuss her metal detector and the endless possibilities of unearthing pirate treasure, but Mathilda was distracted.

'You should see it, Mathilda,' said Olive. 'The whole machine shudders, and it can pick things up miles under the sand.'

'Oh,' said Mathilda and smiled loosely, vaguely, somehow absent.

'And I wanted to ask you about the Christmas concert,' said Olive. 'Mog's organized a dumb dinner with a politician that night, and I was wondering if you'd like to come afterwards. It will be in a restaurant.'

Mathilda liked restaurants. She pronounced it '*restaurong*', like the French and her mum. Dinner in a *restaurong* would be a drawcard for Mathilda.

Mathilda looked at Amelia. Olive looked at Amelia, too. She didn't want to leave anyone out. 'I'm sure Amelia can come along.' Amelia gulped a big nasty laugh and Mathilda went pink.

'Girls, quiet over there,' said Ms Stable-East. 'We require calm to draw.' She tapped a paintbrush against the bobbly sleeve of her hand-knitted jumper for some quiet. It was a shrill-coloured knit, which showed that although Ms Stable-East was the homeroom teacher for Year 7C, she was, first and foremost, a teacher of art.

Olive concentrated on her self-portrait. The face was

too small for the piece of paper on which it floated. Out of the corner of her wide eye, she could see Mathilda and Amelia passing notes backwards and forwards, forwards and back.

When the bell rang for recess, the girls filed out of the Art Cottage. Amelia linked her arm through Mathilda's. 'I'm dying for an ice cream. Got any money?' Amelia ate a Paddle Pop almost every day, but she didn't nibble them like most girls – she ran her finger up along the sides, carving out the ice cream, using her finger like a scoop. Only Amelia Forster could manage to do this elegantly.

'I'll get them. Mog gave me pocket money this morning.' Olive doubted the girls recognized this for the sacrifice it was: as soon as the bell rang for recess or lunch, the tuckshop boiled. The counter was buried under a swarm of grey-and-green jumpers – big girls lounging over it, little kids stuffed under it at awkward angles, the whole woollen mass pushing forwards. Olive would try to punch her way through the crowd, holding her breath. The tuckshop smelled like an old people's home: like canned soup and faded vegetables. Although the snacks were good (especially the cheesy rolls), facing the rabble was never worth it.

Olive faced it anyway, and returned victorious, holding the chocolate Paddle Pops above her head like an Olympic baton. She dropped onto the grass, panting, and smiled. For that plump, perfect second, the three of them were a team.

Amelia peeled off her wrapper and flipped it onto the

ground. The wind blew the paper and it cartwheeled over Olive's shoe. Olive grabbed it.

'Eww, *grow-oss*. Don't pick things off the ground, Olive.' Mathilda and Amelia rolled their eyes and looked at once smug and stern. Olive blushed and dropped the wrapper.

'Olive. Don't litter or we'll all lose house points.' Amelia said this very loudly, in her primmest class-captain voice. She said it so loudly that Ms Stable-East, who was on duty, looked over and frowned.

'Sorry, Ms Stable-East. I'll pick it up,' called Olive.

'*Sorry, Ms Stable-East. I'll pick it up,*' mimicked Amelia and Mathilda in high-pitched, goody-two-shoes voices, and then laughed.

Olive looked at them and squinted, confused. She laughed along with them, but it was clear that she had done something wrong. She was just not entirely sure what.

When the first bell rang, Amelia jumped up and tucked her gummy stick down the back of Olive's collar. Mathilda did too.

'Thanks for the Paddle Pop,' said Amelia. 'C'mon, Till. Let's go to the water fountain before class. Water's good for our pores.'

Till! Olive blinked and waited for Mathilda to say something. Mathilda even made her family call her 'Mathilda' because she thought it sounded more sophisticated.

'Sure, Mill,' said Mathilda. 'My skin's just so *grow-oss*.' Olive stayed seated. *Mill?*

'See ya,' mumbled Mathilda as she turned, more to the Paddle Pop wrapper on the ground than to Olive.

'Bye.' A lot appeared to have changed at the Christmas barbecue picnic. Olive stood and tried to shake the Paddle Pop sticks out of her dress. One was trapped by her belt. Olive's bottom was damp from the grass and she was gritty and sticky. She turned and threaded her way through clusters of sprawled big girls to the loos.

After recess, Year 7C had double Science with Mrs Dixon. Olive was quite fond of Mrs Dixon, although she looked uncannily like a spotted cod (which was, co-incidentally, her species of biological expertise).

Olive was late – it had been harder to scrub her back with paper towel than she'd expected – but Mrs Dixon was too busy writing elements on the board to notice. Around her, the class hummed. Each class had its own tempo, its own pulse. Maths was slow and steady; English was brisk; Science with Mrs Dixon always hummed.

Mathilda and Amelia were wedged together at one end of a bench, whispering. There was a spare seat near them. Olive slid into it. She could feel the eyes of the other girls on her plaits. While she suspected it was already clear to the class that alliances had shifted, Olive couldn't acknowledge it, not yet.

Olive did a quick headcount. There were twenty-three girls in the class – an odd number. One would be left out. The odd one. *Please don't let us do an experiment, please don't let us do an experiment, please don't let us do an experiment*, she prayed.

'OK girls, enough of that,' said Mrs Dixon. 'Get into pairs. We'll be doing an experiment today – the flame experiment. Page seventy-two in your books. Bunsen burners are at the front here.'

The year, Olive noted, was not turning out that well at all.

Olive looked along the bench to Mathilda, who was drawing love hearts around the initials 'J.H.' all over Amelia's pencil case. 'Are you in a pair?' Olive tried to look casual and friendly. Mathilda shrugged a lazy shoulder and turned to Amelia.

'Yep,' said Amelia. She looked straight at Olive with her pretty pretty eyes, waiting for Olive to ask to join them; challenging her to do so. A silence grew on the bench, dividing Olive and Till–Mill. Olive could see it, cold and steely white. She took a breath. Everything smelled like Dettol. 'Um, do you mind if I . . . if I join you?' Olive loathed herself for asking. The silence set.

'Olive Garnaut, get into your lab coat and join in with Amelia and Mathilda, please. We're drastically behind schedule, and we need to get this one out of the way.'

Olive smiled and nodded, although she wanted to scream: *Mrs Dixon, haven't you noticed that Mathilda Graham is* my *partner for experiments? Always? Haven't you noticed that Mathilda Graham is* my *best friend? We're joined at the hip. Isn't it weird that she's with Amelia Forster now and that she's called* Till? But Mrs Dixon was unravelling a pile of Bunsen burner cords.

Amelia lit a match for the flame. 'You can join us.' The match hissed. 'If you want.'

'Sorry,' said Olive.

The girls settled into the experiment and the silence softened. Till–Mill burned chemicals on spoons; Olive recorded the results three times so that they would each have a copy. Olive was neat and industrious; she wanted their notes to be the best. Till–Mill chatted on above her lowered head.

The chatter continued as the girls ate lunch on the oval. Olive chewed at the same patch in her sandwich while Mathilda–Till swooned over the hair of some boy called Angus King. Amelia–Mill promised to put songs on Mathilda–Till's iPod (iPod? Olive hadn't even known Mathilda had one). Mathilda made Amelia–Mill laugh by mimicking a presenter Olive had never even heard of from *Video Hits*. She and Amelia–Mill then repeated the same line from a cartoon, laughing louder each time they said it, trying the words in different voices, shuffling the emphasis.

Olive's sandwich was like plasticine in her mouth. *But this isn't Mathilda. This isn't the* real *Mathilda*, she thought. Olive looked straight at her best friend. She still looked like Mathilda – not like Till at all. The real Mathilda just had to be in there somewhere.

After they had eaten, Mathilda and Amelia leaped up as if on an invisible cue. Olive stuffed the rest of her sandwich in its bag and stood, too. Till–Mill took off across the oval. Olive trailed a pace behind them like one of the deferential Chinese wives they had learned about from the olden days.

Till–Mill talked on and on about the Christmas barbecue picnic, a saucepan of stars and James Hurley's *hilarious jokes*. Olive stared at Amelia's baggy jumper, which hooked down under her bottom, and at her perfectly straight north–south parting. It was hard to compete with a parting like that.

Olive tried to pull her own jumper sleeves down over her wrists. Her jumper was shorter than Amelia's and Mathilda's. Olive had never really noticed before.

'C'mon, Till. Let's go to the Art Cottage,' said Amelia.

'Sure, Mill,' said Mathilda.

Olive spun on her heels and dutifully followed the perfect parting, but she was getting angry. What was Amelia doing? Mathilda Graham and her entire family and their chairs *in chintz* and date scones were Olive's. Just Olive's.

When they got to the Art Cottage, Amelia looked over her shoulder and announced a little too loudly, 'C'mon, *Till*. Let's go to the netball courts.' The Till–Mill duo turned. Olive followed, bringing up the rear.

Amelia–Mill chatted on about the cricket and membership and how she would see if there was a spare ticket this weekend so that Mathilda–Till could come and sit with her family and maybe even see James Hurley and Angus King.

'Cricket? I didn't know you even *liked* cricket, Mathilda,' said Olive. She dug her nails into her palms. The comment had slid out. It sounded much more sarcastic than she'd intended, aggressive even.

Amelia looked at Mathilda. 'Did you hear something?' she asked. Mathilda laughed.

'I'm not sure if I *heard* something, but I definitely *smell* something,' continued Amelia, shooting Olive another quick look over her shoulder. She might as well have used a bazooka. Olive stopped. She waited for Mathilda to leap to her defence – surely this time Amelia had gone too far – but Mathilda just poked her T-bar in the dust, making a wall to block a stream of ants.

Olive turned deep red and started sweating. Blood hurtled around her body and clogged her ears. Everything was fuzzy. The light refracted; all the pale things appeared so bright that they hurt, and all the dark things looked like one thick smudge of deepest darkest ebony. Olive concentrated on keeping her head upright and turned away. She blurred her vision so that the hyperdark superlight didn't hurt.

Don't let them see me cry. Don't let them see me cry. Just to the loos. You'll get to the loos, she said to herself, walking methodically with a tight face and as much dignity as she could muster. Two paces from the cubicle, Olive crumpled, bereft.

Sticks and stones may break my bones but words will never hurt me, Olive repeated to herself that afternoon in English, over and over. *Silly kids' mantra*. Any fool knew that, pound for pound, words could pack as much punch as stone. Whenever she felt teary, Olive groped around the inside of her desk, pretending to look for something essential in its deepest corners. She bit the inside of her mouth until it hurt.

Olive sat, an island surrounded by a stretch of cream linoleum. There was nobody near her; nobody wanted to be. That was the thing about being dumped: it was contagious. Schoolgirls hunted in packs. Olive was so contagious she could almost see her own disease.

At the back of the room, Mathilda–Till tipped her chair against the wall, balancing. She chortled loudly, playing up, showing off. She was performing for Amelia like a Sea World seal. At first Olive had thought that Mathilda–Till was pretending. She realized now that Mathilda had had all these interests stored up – iPods and *Video Hits* and boys and pores – and Olive hadn't noticed.

Conversations bubbled on around Olive. She listened. Mathilda was not the only one. Somehow the rules had changed, and it seemed that every other girl in the class had read the new book and was on top of it. Every girl except Olive.

Olive concentrated on a design she was looping about her spelling. She could hear both Mathilda and Amelia laughing now – talking and laughing. Talking and laughing about her.

'You know, Mum says that if she had a father she'd be a different person. She reckons she'd be normal. You know, normal on the inside as well,' stage-whispered Mathilda across the room.

'She's not *that* normal on the outside.'

Olive looked round to see Amelia sprinkle dimples

about the room like fairy dust. She pressed her hands against her ears to block Till–Mill out, and bit harder and harder on the inside of her mouth, waiting for the day to end. Wherever she looked, girls ducked her stare or squinted, feigning short-sightedness.

When the bell finally clanged, Olive picked up her bag and exited quickly, head high, rigid inside her blazer. The pool of checked uniforms parted to let her through.

Olive left without looking back at the new Till again.

7
The Twenty-second Day of the Month

Olive walked fast. 'I'll show them, bloody bloody. I'll show them, bloody Till bloody Mill,' she muttered, stomping down the pavement towards the beach. 'How dare they, bum and bugger, how dare they.'

This was the worst day of Olive's entire life. It was the twenty-second day of November. Olive kicked out at a picket fence. More twos. No surprises there.

Olive was working herself up into what Mog termed a Right Tizz. 'I am a middle-pick girl,' she spat. And she was. She was the kind of girl who was consistently class vice-captain in third term or class captain in fourth term. Never a leader, but certainly never picked last in PE. She was no Nut Allergy. Nut Allergy had matted hair and she stank. In junior school she wet her pants, and sometimes, on hot afternoons, her uniform had been so damp that it had actually steamed. These days, she was always stranded on the oval when every other girl in the class had been snaffled for netball teams.

'I do not smell,' said Olive, unconvinced. Perhaps she just hadn't noticed? People didn't. When she thought about it, every family had a smell. Mathilda smelled like the Graham family home: all beeswax polish and baking. Amelia smelled like apple shampoo, washing detergent and new leather.

Maybe Olive smelled like her home too, and she just hadn't noticed. Maybe Olive smelled like knick-knacks – like old costumes and second-hand books.

Olive flipped Mathilda's words over in her mind, like sausages in a pan. *Mum says that if she had a father she'd be a different person. She'd be normal.* She kicked a can in the gutter. Till–Mill were right. Mog and Olive were just not normal. The can reverberated back onto Olive's shoe. She crushed it.

If WilliamPetersMustardSeed was here, I'd be normal. If WilliamPetersMustardSeed was here, my family would be like the Grahams and I wouldn't be so strange. If WilliamPetersMustardSeed was here, I'd wish for things that would fit on eyelashes, too. It was so obvious. Olive couldn't believe it hadn't occurred to her before. She ran across the road, ashamed and angry.

A new sign had been erected in the beach car park.

SEASIDE CITY COUNCIL – UPCOMING EVENT
THE BEACH WILL BE CLOSED BETWEEN WOLF LANE
AND KELSO PIER FROM 22 NOVEMBER – 2 DECEMBER IN
PREPARATION FOR THE INAUGURAL SEASIDE CARNIVAL

AND SAND SCULPTURE DISPLAY BIENNALE.
LICENSED FISHERMEN EXEMPT.
PARKING RESTRICTIONS WILL APPLY.
GO TO WWW.SEASIDECITYCOUNCIL.VIC.GOV.AU FOR
MORE INFORMATION.

Olive kicked the sign. Now the council had stolen her beach?

Olive wanted to throw her head back and howl. She wanted to wail. Everything was spinning, spiralling out of control. She threw her bag down on the pavement. Something a little longer than a lipstick fell out of the front pocket and rattle-rolled across the concrete. The something stopped at Olive's shoe.

Olive bent down to pick up the Brass Eye. It must have been in her bag since their last Science project. She looked through it at the beach and then down at the self-portrait which was unfurling in the top of her bag where she had stuffed it. The portrait swooped into view, doubling as it uncurled. Olive shoved the Brass Eye in her pocket. She didn't have the patience for it right now. She needed to stretch, to move, to feel the sea – even if the council was trying to keep her from it.

It was a grey day, but the beach was busy. Thickset men in orange trousers were unloading crates from trucks onto the sand. There was a lot of shouting, heave-hoing and whistling through fingers. Olive peeled off her shoes and socks, stuffed them in her school bag and jumped down onto the beach. She wove her way between the boxes, feeling the sand break into biscuits under her feet. The Brass Eye bumped against her thigh and the salted air soothed her. Before long, Olive's breath had steadied.

The tide was low, and the hide of a sandbar lolling just off the beach parted the water. Fishermen in gumboots drew sluggish nets through the shallows. Chipped shells and threads of kelp lay in bands along the shore, mapping the paths of the most curious waves.

Olive walked along the water's edge, tracing one shell-line all the way to Kelso Pier before it tapered out. That far away, the mob of men and crates had also thinned, and there were only a few coils of rope laying claim to the sand.

Olive looked back at her footprints. She had read that in Antarctica, when it stormed, the wind blew away everything but the compressed snow in people's foot-prints. Those inverse footprints then stood high, like footprint-shaped snowmen. Olive thought there was something very majestic about that – something very grand about being the sort of person who didn't leave a dent, but left a peak instead.

A wave spread over the beach. Olive ran up under the pier to avoid it. Through the slats above her head, she could see shifting clouds. To the right, the beach arched back towards home in a fawn bow, speckled with far-away men. Her view to the left was, however, impeded – blocked by a row of silver-backed boards. It was weird – it looked as if someone had boarded up the pier on one side. Olive ducked back out into the afternoon light to investigate.

They were not, in fact, boards but vast mirrors that had been propped up against the pier. There were three of them all together: three carnival mirrors with luscious gilt frames. The sand on which they were standing was hidden under a braid of torn rugs and twine. Next to the mirrors was a cool box with a sticker reading PROPERTY OF SEASIDE CITY COUNCIL.

Olive stepped in front of the first mirror and smiled. She looked like a Coke bottle – long and elongated at the top, swollen and stumpy at the bottom. She jumped across to the second. It was even worse – she was as skinny as a chopstick and as tall as a skyscraper. It was a strange thing seeing herself distorted like that. Olive couldn't stop looking at her wide eyes. They seemed to be the only parts of her body that were anchored as her flesh contorted about them.

Olive stepped in front of the last mirror and started. Its surface was almost alive; it was like looking up, through goggles, at the silvered underbelly of the sea's skin. Olive's reflection rode on crests across the face of the glass, breaking into pieces if she moved even the tiniest inch. She held her breath. The mirror swirled and twirled, flickering with fragments of splintered rainbow and molten silver, pulling and warping her body. Even her irises dissolved into watery spirals. It was as if she had melted, melted into a pool of liquid crystal and molten glass.

Olive rolled the Brass Eye between her fingers. It was still in her pocket; she'd been gripping it without realizing and the stem was warm. Looking into the third mirror was not unlike looking through the Brass Eye; it was just as mesmerizing, as fluid and alive. Olive was as moved as she had been when she first sank her fingers into Mrs Graham's wedding dress. 'It's beautiful,' she said out loud.

Olive trained the Brass Eye tentatively on the mirror. She expected the mirror to boil. She expected a spectacular display – to be dazzled with sparks, if not live flames. The light, however, refracted, and Olive's reflection congealed. Her silhouette hovered in the circle of the Brass Eye, forming and then fading, forming and then fading, evoking things in Olive that she couldn't describe but somehow knew.

Olive felt giddy, weightless. She lowered the Brass Eye and put it back in her pocket. The mirror changed again. While it still shimmered, the swaying had steadied, and she appeared not once, but twice. One of the reflected heads in the mirror turned. Behind her, something stirred.

Olive spun. A kid stood right next to her, shaking water from its arms. They were pale, skinny arms – arms that would burn in two minutes at the beach. The arms were attached to a girl with long blonde hair that hung and swung; a peculiar girl who looked ever so slightly like an extraterrestrial: a very pale extraterrestrial. A girl with shins the exact colour of chicken loaf.

Olive tried to breathe in, but she couldn't. She dropped into a crouch on the sand – just shrivelled up and retracted like the sea anemones that she and Mog found (and poked their fingers into) in rock pools down the coast. Olive shivered and looked up again. The girl's mouth wound into a smile.

'What are you doing?' The girl jiggled her arms and legs. 'Man, I'm so wet, I could get part-time work as a water feature.'

Olive didn't answer. Her underarms were damp. She could smell the stress in her sweat; it clung to the air like Mog's sweat clung to her shirts in court. The girl cocked her head and peered at Olive. She tapped Olive's forehead with her fist. 'Hello in there? Anyone home?'

Olive looked around for help, or at the very least an explanation. None was forthcoming. She peeped up at the girl, who had one hand on her hip.

'And you are?' The girl's voice was as high as Olive's.

Olive stood, clutching the Brass Eye in one hand and a tuft of her uniform in the other. 'Confused,' she said. 'Actually, very confused.'

The girl reached out her hand. 'Hello, Very Confused, I'm Pip. Pip Garnaut.'

Olive couldn't help but smile. 'I'm a Garnaut too, but Olive.' As Olive reached out her own hand, the girls' finely veined wrists bumped together. They both snatched them back. Pip laughed.

If she had let herself think it (which was a big *if* for a glass-half-empty type of person), Olive Garnaut might have realized, as early as that moment, that she was no longer an only child.

8
Curiouser and Curiouser

Pip and Olive sat on the sand in front of the row of mirrors. Olive snuck peeks at Pip. Pip stared straight at Olive. They were so extraordinarily identical that Olive couldn't tell Arthur from Martha, as Mog would say. She scanned Pip's face for differentiations – odd spots, dimples, cowlicks – but there was nothing. Things on Pip weren't even back-to-front like in a normal reflection. The two girls were peas in a pod – they even distorted in the mirrors in exactly the same manner.

'We're pretty similar,' said Olive after a while.

'Yes,' said Pip. 'I expect we're twins.'

'Twins? But—' Olive quivered.

'What?'

'But I don't have any siblings.'

'Look at us. We must be.' Pip rolled her eyes. 'We even have the same surname.'

This extreme change of circumstance was difficult to digest. Although Olive wanted to refute it, the evidence was right there in front of her nose; the very same nose as Pip's.

Before them, the third mirror glimmered. 'It's like a pool of sparkles,' said Olive, attempting to get back onto more certain terrain. As soon as she'd spoken, she felt like an idiot.

If she looked like one, Pip didn't notice. 'It is pretty beautiful.'

Olive panned for more things to say, but it was awkward. There were no rules. Mrs Graham said that etiquette was always there to guide you; to make people feel comfortable in every situation. She even had a book on it, on the top shelf in her kitchen. Although the book instructed *one* how to use a fish knife, and which way to pass somebody at the theatre, Olive couldn't imagine that it covered situations like this; situations like *Suggested Introductory Conversation Topics for One and One's Newly Discovered Twin.*

While Olive struggled, however, Pip didn't seem to need a book. She seemed perfectly comfortable.

'I'm thirsty.' Pip stood up and walked over to the cool box. The pillar it sat next to stood out because it was bent. 'Crooked as an old man's elbow,' said Pip. She lifted the lid and rifled through the ice. 'Beer, beer, beer, gross, gross, gross, Red Bull, Red Bull, Double Yoke Eggnog. That will do.'

'I'm not sure we should touch that. It's not ours.'

'I'm parched. Open this, can you?'

Olive opened a carton and Pip glugged the milkshake down. 'Try it,' she gargled, pearls of milk spotting in the corners of her mouth.

Olive was a picky eater who stuck to Brands She Knew. Double Yoke Eggnog was not a Brand She Knew, or even a Brand She'd Heard Of, but stress had left Olive dying of thirst, and people dying of thirst were not in any position to be picky. Besides, she didn't want Pip to think she was a chicken, not on their first day.

Olive looked around to make sure there were no workmen in sight and opened the top of the carton. She was a bit worried that Double Yoke Eggnog might be exactly the sort of thing she'd suspected Okey Doke would serve (when in actual fact he always stuck to passion fruit and raspberry). But the drink smelled all right – well, it didn't smell of anything obviously disgusting, like blood 'n' bone or alfalfa. Olive crinkled her face and took a tiny sip. Despite her anxiety, Double Yoke Eggnog was delicious.

Pip started on a second carton and burped without apologizing. Her burp smelled. 'This is *eggsellent*,' she said.

'That's a terrible pun.' It was as lousy as any of Mr Graham's. It was the sort of bad pun that would have made Mathilda roll her eyes and squawk 'Da-aaad' like a banshee (or so Mr Graham said) before she clubbed him over the shoulder. Olive liked bad puns – they were about as dad as chuckles, shaving cream and polo shirts. Olive would never have expected a twin to pun.

'So, what are these mirrors for?' Pip tossed the

Double Yoke Eggnog carton and it spun away in a plume of milk.

Olive watched the carton nosedive into the sand. 'I'm not sure. I was going to ask you the same thing – you're the one who emerged through them. I'd assumed they were for the festival.'

'I did not emerge through them.' Pip chewed the words, exaggerating Olive's prim schoolgirl vowels. Olive winced. Pip wiped the back of her hand along her mouth, smearing rather than cleaning her face. 'Let's go,' she said, dropping back to her normal voice. 'I'm starving and I want to get out of here before my stomach corrodes. Woman can only live on Double Yoke Eggnog for so long.' Pip stood up. She held out two hands. 'Well, come on. Are you both coming?'

'Both?' Olive turned round. Surely one double was enough for the afternoon. That was going to take enough explaining as it was. Thankfully, though, there were no more chicken-loaf shins in sight. 'Who else are you inviting?!'

Pip looked straight at Olive with her pale eyes. 'You you both both.'

Oh man, thought Olive. Maybe Pip was seeing double. Maybe that was some weird spin-off of this cloning process, or whatever on earth it was.

Olive held up three fingers. 'How many?'

'Six six.'

Olive's stomach clenched. She hadn't asked for this whole thing, and what if now she was stuck with a freak for a twin? What if that wasn't the only thing wrong with

Pip? What if things were wrong with her on the inside, too? What if, say, she had two pancreases? What if she didn't have two lungs but four? Would that make her more likely to die of a fatal asthma attack, or half as likely? Would she start fitting in the classroom?

Olive's mind whirled through a list of possible but dire outcomes. Pip winked. 'Tricked you,' she said and laughed like a hyena. She bent over, cackling so hard that she had to hold her stomach.

Olive stood slowly, a bit peeved. It wasn't *that* funny. Pip spied Olive's pout from the side. 'If you're not careful, a bird will come and perch on that lip.' Pip laughed more.

That was exactly the sort of thing Olive's gran used to say to tease her, and it had always made her blood boil. Olive was tempted to walk right off and leave Pip stranded on the beach, four-lunged and starving or not, but Pip smiled her big wobbly smile.

'Sorry,' she said.

Olive forgave her instantly.

Suddenly, there was a shout from somewhere down near the shore. A workman with furry shoulders gestured at the girls. 'Oi,' he called. 'You there. Beach is strictly outta bounds – and if you've gone anywhere near that cool box, I'll tan ya.' He started walking towards them on legs so chunky they joined all the way down to the knee. A heeler dog with slack blue gums trotted beside him. Olive froze.

Pip giggled. 'Crap,' she said. 'Let's get out of here.' She sprinted up the beach towards the footpath. Olive grabbed her school bag, then began collecting the empty cartons Pip had tossed.

'Olive, are you nuts? This is no time for tidy town. He said he'd *tan* us,' Pip called back.

Olive looked round. The furry man and his heeler had launched into a jog. They lumbered towards her, sand churning beneath their feet. Up closer, the dog looked more dingo than heeler.

'Olive, *quick*.'

'Blow this,' said Olive and, dumping the rubbish, she sprinted after Pip.

9
Crime and In-tu-ition

It took Olive a while to catch Pip. She'd taken off along the beach path that headed back towards home, apparently unhampered by the Double Yoke Eggnog, which was sloshing about Olive's own tummy and giving her a stitch.

'Did you lose him?' Pip panted, slowing to a walk.

'Yep.' Olive shuddered at the thought of the slack-gummed dingo.

'So, what took you so long?' Pip looked down at Olive's pigeon toe. 'Man, if you'd just walk normally, you'd go faster. What's with the bird feet?' She started to run again.

Olive sniffed, re-aligned her toes (somewhere closer to first position) and followed.

At the end of the path, the beach car park basked in

the evening sun. A flag advertising drinks cracked in the breeze.

'Do you like ice cream?' asked Olive.

'Of course.'

'I'll show you Okey Doke's, then. He's just across there.'

Parked in front of them was an old purple van with sloppy flowers and the words ADDICTION TO DRUGS SHOWS COMMITMENT painted on the side.

'Mog, our mum, used to have one of those vans, with a bed inside and wind chimes hanging from the rear-view mirror,' said Olive. 'I've seen the pictures. Mog said she could start it with a spoon in the ignition. Whenever WilliamPetersMustardSeed – that's our dad – lost the keys, it didn't matter. They just worked their way through the cutlery drawer using everything but the Good Silver.'

Olive looked around. Behind them, two girls in Joanne d'Arc uniforms were walking towards the car park: one had a long blonde ponytail; the other a surge of dark curls. Their heads were bowed in an arc of confidentiality.

Olive felt sick. What were they doing here? Okey Doke was hers. She'd introduced Mathilda to him. Olive watched the girls grow as they drew closer. Pip jiggled the handle of the van. 'It's open.'

'Let's see if this one's the same as Mog's,' Olive said quickly.

'Are you serious? You didn't strike me as the type.'

'Just hurry.' Olive opened the front door and jumped up inside.

The van seats were sun-warm and the ashtray was crammed with cigarette butts that smelled sweet, like allspice. Pip rifled through old bottles of sunscreen, broken mozzie coils and half-tubes of Life Savers that she found on the shelf under the dashboard. Olive angled the rearvision mirror so that she could see Till–Mill through the back window.

'What are you doing?' Pip asked.

'Nothing.' Olive watched the reflected girls as they approached, talking and laughing, without hats or blazers.

Pip offered Olive a Life Saver. 'They're not too stale.'

'No.' Olive shook her head. 'No thanks.' She laced her fingers.

Pip squinted and clambered over the seat into the back. Olive kept her eye on the mirror. When the Joanne d'Arc girls were almost at the van, their faces fell into focus.

'Thankyouthankyouthankyou.' Olive sank against the seat as two Year 9 girls headed towards the beach. It was not Till–Mill at all.

Pip crawled back into the front. 'You look pretty comfortable for a person who was so anxious thirty seconds ago.'

Olive smiled. 'OK, let's go.'

'All right. There's not so much as a chopstick back here anyway. Hang on.' Pip had spotted something down the side of the front seat. 'What about that!'

'This?' Olive held up a barbecue prong.

'Brilliant, let's try it. You hop down and do the pedals. I'll do the wheel.'

Although Pip was arguably Olive's twin, she was already displaying the bossy older-sister tendencies Mathilda showed with her younger brothers.

'No way, Pip. It's totally illegal.' Bossiness didn't really bother Olive, but criminality did, and while Olive may have survived drinking a Brand She Had Never Heard Of, and escaped a furry workman, not to mention his dingo, driving someone else's van was surely inviting arrest.

'Don't worry about it,' said Pip. 'We won't go far. Anyway, it might not even start.'

'All right, all right.' Olive knelt on the floor. She pushed an old flip-flop under the seat with her fingertip and wrinkled her nose. She could see the imprint of somebody's sweaty foot on it, including a knobbly bunion on the side. It was disgusting. Olive looked at the pedals; there were three. All three were dirty. She tried not to think of the knobbly bunion on them.

'OK, keep your head down or the wheel might decapitate you. Let's start it.' Pip leaned over Olive and wedged the barbecue prong in the ignition. It glided in, and when she turned it, the van coughed.

'Bingo-bango.'

'Pip, stop.' Olive jumped back up onto the seat, just as the engine stalled.

Pip released the handbrake. The van rolled forwards.

'Whoo hoo! We're outta here. Wheeeeeeeeeeeeeeee,' trilled Pip out of the window. She was perched up, on her knees, leaning forwards while she concentrated. Her blonde hair was plastered to her face in stringy bits and her face was flushed. Olive could see the muscles in her sister's puny arms straining as she tried to harness the half-ton of purple lead and rubber. It was terrifying and exhilarating.

'OK, Olive,' yelled Pip. 'Let's get up some pace.'

'Pip, no.' Olive pulled the handbrake up as hard as she could. The van crunched.

'Crap.'

The girls had rolled about four metres and were now pulled up against a strip of salty native grasses and a rubbish bin.

'Guess we'll have to go out the window,' said Pip as she wound it down. Head first, she commando-rolled out. Olive toppled after her.

'Cow-jumped-over-the-moon-geek-knickers,' shrieked Pip, spotting Olive's undies. The problem with not having grown one single centimetre since Grade 4 was that one ended up with a bottom the size of a Grade 4, which could be extremely limiting. Amelia, on the other hand, had a size-eight ladies' bum and knickers with broderie anglaise trim in ivory.

'You're probably wearing them, too,' retorted Olive indignantly.

Pip checked. 'Crap.'

Olive couldn't help noticing that Pip swore like a trooper. Mrs Graham said that people only swore when their vocabularies were inadequate to deal with their emotions. Although Olive didn't like to think of Pip as inadequate, she did hope that swearing wasn't contagious.

Before Olive could ponder this too long, Pip whipped her knickers off and threw them into the bin next to the van.

'Nobody's catching me in those.'

'You can't do that,' cried Olive, realizing that her twin's behaviour might explain why there were always pairs of soggy knickers at the beach. Olive had never been able to work out how so many people could collectively forget their underwear.

'I can.' Pip bounded towards the shop.

'Pip,' called Olive, completely scandalized by her sister's bare bottom under an already transparent uniform. Pip responded to Olive's prudishness by doing a cartwheel, right there in the middle of the car park. She then spun round and kept running towards Okey Doke's, drunk on adrenalin.

Olive, abandoning all sense of propriety, followed.

The ice cream at Okey Doke's was piled high in folds and teemed with shattered honeycomb, thick chocolate curls, or whole rosy strawberries. *The softa the nice cream the quicka to eat*, Okey Doke said when people commented on the texture of his fare.

Pip threaded her arm through Olive's at the counter. The girls pushed their noses against the glass and watched while Okey Doke's chubby wrists ladled ice cream into lacy cones. Although it was not far off closing time, the crowd was five people deep. Olive caught Pip's eye and nodded towards the door; Pip slipped outside to wait.

Olive knew Pip would want to check out the bug-catcher at the entrance. She could hear it from inside the shop, electrocuting insects with a crack as they flew into the blue light. Besides, Olive didn't want to run the risk of old Okey Doke having a heart attack when he realized that he was serving his fine upstanding ice cream to a schoolgirl with no knickers.

'One scoop of raspberry and one of passion fruit on a waffle cone, please.' Olive paused. 'And I'll also have a scoop of raspberry and one of honey.'

'Okey doke, artichoke,' the man responded on cue. He looked up at Olive. 'Two at once, bella?'

'The second's for my sister,' said Olive. 'You haven't met her yet, but she's actually my twin sister.' Okey Doke raised an eyebrow. Olive panicked. For one moment she thought he'd guessed that it was Pip who had started the van with a barbecue prong and was currently cavorting with dead bugs and no underpants. If he did, however, he didn't comment.

Outside the shop, Olive handed Pip her ice cream.

'Wicked. Hey, check this out.' Pip pitched a stick into the bug-catcher. It exploded in a strip of sparks, then dissolved in a curl of smoke. The ash gathered on the fried insect carcasses in the tray. The bug-catcher was certainly dramatic.

The girls started on their cones, both eating the ice cream in small bites. Pip eyed Olive's cone. 'I hate passion-fruit pips – they get stuck in my teeth.'

'That's weird,' said Olive. 'I didn't ask you what flavours you wanted, because I knew. I knew you'd want honey and raspberry, just like I knew why you'd want to wait outside. It's like I've known all the way along.'

Pip shrugged. 'You didn't *know* I'd cartwheel without knickers.'

'No,' admitted Olive.

Pip took another bite of her ice cream. 'You should have seen your face. Classic. Besides,' she continued, 'it's not the same as *knowing* I'm about to be brutalized by a fifty-foot fanged turtle and risking all to come to my rescue.'

'I guess not,' said Olive, who didn't actually know what 'brutalized' meant, but thought it sounded horrible. 'But fifty-foot fanged turtle or not, it's *in-tu-ition*, Pip. It's just the same as the circus horses the morning before the dust storm.'

Pip traced a line in the pile of ash under the bug-catcher with a stick and looked bored. Olive persevered. 'Ms Stable-East told us about this dust storm that rolled in years ago and dumped a thick blanket of red dirt all over the city. She thought it was the end of the world, but the thing that's stuck in her mind is the circus horses she saw on the telly.'

'What was with them?' Pip appeared to have no interest in teachers or *in-tu-ition* but a little more interest in circus horses.

'Well, the entire morning before the storm, the horses were upset. They had dry noses, and they tugged at their harnesses, kicking at the ground until their hooves bled. It's like they knew it was coming. Ms Stable-East says that sometimes animals just know things – know things that we don't.'

'So, I don't get it.'

'She says we should never forget that we're mammals too.' Olive laughed. 'Mathilda reckons Ms Stable-East says that to justify her hairy legs and moustache. She's a beast.' Olive gnawed her bottom lip. 'But what if she's actually a bit right? Perhaps I *knew* what flavour you wanted because I'm a mammal.'

'Could be.' Pip lobbed her cone into the bug-catcher. 'But she should wax. Whales are mammals, and they don't go around with hairy lips.' The cone exploded into sparks. 'Who's this Mathilda, anyway?'

'My best friend,' said Olive. 'She and Amelia Forster and me are a threesome.' The lie tugged.

Pip poked some ash on the ground. Her feet were turned out like a piano's.

'Don't worry. I'm sure you can join in.'

'Whatever.' Pip blew the end of the stick. Olive wondered how she could not care.

The fluorescent light above their heads spluttered again. Olive stood up. 'Good-o. I hadn't realized it was so late. We should get going.'

Olive loved the phrase 'Good-o'. It sounded very efficient and very mature. Mrs Graham pronounced it so that the 'o' was about twice as long as the 'good'. Olive did too. Pip didn't move.

'We should probably go pr-pr-pronto.' Olive wasn't very good at rolled 'r's. Pip stared but didn't move.

'C'mon, Pip. Mog might get home soon, and we've got

heaps to organize before tomorrow.' Pip stretched slowly and rolled her eyes.

Olive rolled her eyes back. If one thing was certain, eyes were easier to roll than 'r's.

10
The 'I' in We

Pip and Olive walked home. A group of boys with dusty school shoes and hot chips were sprawled over Mrs Stewart's fence on the corner of Olive's street. As the girls walked past the hot-chip boys, Olive put her head down. Her hand shot up to her forehead and she pretended to scratch a mozzie bite. It was a habit she'd assumed ever since one of the boys had commented on the size of her forehead a couple of weeks ago. 'Egghead', he'd called her.

Pip stared directly at the tangle of school shoes and caps. 'What a bunch of off-chops.'

'Shush,' said Olive, looking over her shoulder to make sure the hot-chip boys hadn't heard; and if they had heard, that they didn't care; and if they had heard and did care, that they weren't going to clobber them. But the boys were talking and smoking and laughing and couldn't have looked less interested in the twins.

A square of footpath in front of Olive's house had been roped off.

'Hey, concrete! Let's check if it's still wet.' Pip crouched down and stuck her finger in. It was.

'Do you think you should?' Olive asked dubiously. She was learning swiftly that she was not as inclined to crime as her sister.

'What? You'd pass up a patch as fresh as this? Are you kidding?' Pip ran her finger through the cement. It looked as thick and grainy as biscuit dough. 'Perfect consistency.'

OLIVE, wrote Pip.

'You *can't* do that. That's outrageous,' said Olive. 'Mog will see it and freak. And she'll think it was me.'

Olive looked back at the hot-chip boys. They were flicking stones at a lamppost. Apart from that, the street was empty.

Olive added:

   P

OLIVE

   P

'Or she'll think it was you,' Olive giggled. 'Look. It joins with the "i" in me.'

'The "i" in we, you mean.' Pip stood up. The twins walked through Olive's front gate and down the side path to the back door. For the first time ever, Olive didn't notice the branches and their long twiggy fingers.

'You got anything to eat? I'm starving.' Pip headed straight to the fridge and opened the door. Although it was the first time she'd done this, there was already a sense of habit about her action.

Olive pulled the Sultana Bran down from the cupboard, together with two bowls and a can of strawberry Nesquik. She nudged Pip out of the way and fetched the milk from the fridge, sniffing it first like Mrs Graham. It smelled a bit off, but milk always smelled a bit off, so Olive poured it into a gravy boat (which was practically a milk jug) and mixed some Nesquik in. The girls sat down to big bowls of cereal and strawberry milk.

'Gross,' said Pip. 'Sultanas. I hate sultanas. Wrinkly rabbit turds.' Pip began extracting the sultanas from her bowl and putting them on the table, where they joined Olive's in a wrinkly rabbit-turd mountain.

'Why's this so scrunched?' Pip had picked Olive's self-portrait from the top of her school bag and smoothed it out on the table. The face was still too small for the piece of paper on which it floated. Olive grabbed it from her.

'Don't. It's dreadful,' she muttered, crumpling the picture and grinding it into the palm of her hand. She was embarrassed Pip had seen it. It was like somebody seeing something private – knickers with a poo-streak or worm tablets at summer camp.

'It looked OK to me. Well, obviously until you destroyed it.'

Olive took a breath and concentrated on pulling together a smile. 'Would you like a tour?' she asked in her brightest kitchen-wipe voice.

The girls pushed through the house. Pip barged in front of her sister, squealing as she bumped into the piles of knick-knacks. Olive ran behind her, trying to steady the towers of junk. Those she couldn't save toppled with a thud, taking others down in their wake like massive dominoes. Dust ballooned up in clouds, glinting in the light.

'Watch it.' Olive was starting to think about the logistics of having somebody to stay. The house was big, but with all of Mog's stuff, there wasn't much room left.

Pip looked around at the chaos. 'Why doesn't Mog have a servant or something? You know, a cleaner or even a nanny?'

'For political reasons. I did actually have a babysitter ages ago, but it didn't work out.'

Olive's babysitter had been called Sarah Afar. Sarah Afar couldn't drive, and she'd hated Olive almost as much as she'd hated public transport. Sarah was a student and a D-grade actor. The first time she babysat Olive, she had hobbled in the front door scrunched over a walking cane. Olive was appalled.

Mog had looked at Olive's stricken face and mouthed the words 'method actor' over Sarah's shoulder. Olive had laughed. She knew all about method actors from Mog. They were actors who got themselves so wrapped up in their roles that they behaved like the person they were playing, twenty-four seven. The end result was that Olive never knew what Sarah Afar would be like – it depended entirely on what play she was in.

'A-tchooooooooo. Aaaaa-tchoooooooo,' sneezed Pip from the billiard room. 'Check this out.'

Olive made her way over to Pip, whose face

was hidden under the lip of a velvet riding hat.

'That's Mog.' Olive pointed to a poster leaning up against a stack of boxes. In it, Mog was dressed in a turban, her skin stained blue like the god Krishna. Her eyes looked big and navy. Olive loved it because Mog looked so flamboyant. She had been an actor in her student days, and posters from the plays in which she had featured – some framed, some unframed, all sticky with dust – lined the hall.

'Wow,' said Pip. 'She's so beautiful.'

'I know. She's a bit wacko, but she can be fun.'

Pip took the riding hat off her head and wrapped a gold-threaded sari around her neck. Silk billowed behind her. She flapped a straw around her face and pretended to suck on it like a cigarette in a holder. 'Ahh, darlink.' Pip sniffed artfully. 'Mmmmmm, place those roses with the others in my changing room. Oh, and fetch me a martini – generous on the gin, light on the olives.'

Olive smiled.

In the evening light, Pip looked strange, but it wasn't only the sari silk. At first they had seemed a perfect double, and Olive had thought Pip could be her doppelgänger – go to school in her place, go to the dentist, go to swimming lessons – but now Olive suspected that people might actually guess.

The harder you looked, the more different they were. Put simply, Pip was the same but better: her eyes looked bigger and somehow less weirdly spaced; her skin was not as blotchy; she seemed taller, stronger and, well, plain prettier.

It was like when Olive bought two Caramello Koalas – one was always superior, even if they came out of the same mould in the same factory. If Olive and Pip were Caramello Koalas, thought Olive, then there was no doubt that Olive had less caramel.

Olive looked from Pip back to the poster of Mog. Mog! Olive had completely forgotten to call her.

Trudy answered the phone. 'I'll put you through, Olive,' she squawked, 'but I should warn you, things are feverish in here.'

'Hi, Ol, how was your day?' spurted Mog onto the line.

'Fine, thanks. Crazy. You'll never guess what happened. I went to the beach and they were putting up some sculpture carnival thing, but I saw this set of mirrors against Kelso Pier, a—'

'Yes, I understand the importance of this mediation, James, but I am on the phone to my daughter. I shall be in again shortly. Sorry, Ol. That man. Where were you?'

'I took the Brass Eye, and . . . to trim a long story, I was doubled – well, twinned – and now Pip is—'

'Yes, James, as I *just* explained not less than twenty-three seconds ago, I'm coming. Sorry, Ol. Things are frantic here. There's enormous pressure to find a solution tonight, and everyone's as tense as ticks. All right if I see you later at home? Tuck yourself up with a hottie. Love you.' The phone clicked.

'And I can't wait for you to meet her,' said Olive into the dead line.

❊   ❊   ❊

Olive ploughed through the debris created by her sister and went to find some linen.

'Mog will be home later.'

'Wicked,' yelled Pip from Olive's room and sneezed again.

'Much later,' said Olive into the hall cupboard.

When she returned, Pip had picked up Olive's watch and was buckling it around her wrist using the last, homemade hole. It was the special watch Mog had bought Olive for her first double-digit birthday, and Olive was careful not to wear it in the shower. Pip held up her hand. 'That's nice.'

Olive's eyes moved between her sister's wrist and the watch-shaped gap in her jewellery box.

Pip scanned Olive's CDs and DVDs. '*The Little Mermaid*? Isn't that for kids?'

'It's Disney's best,' said Olive and stopped. She loved Disney's animations. She'd watched *The Little Mermaid* DVD until it got lines in it.

Pip went back to the CDs and DVDs. 'Nothing I like.' She switched on the radio and turned the volume up.

'Lucky Mog's not home with a gin-and-tonic hang-over,' Olive said pointedly.

'What's the fish's name?' A fish the colour of canned tomato soup spiralled up and down a bowl.

'Ariel,' said Olive, hoping Pip would fail to recognize the obvious Disney reference.

'I'd have called him Killer.' Pip sashayed over to Olive's cupboard, bobbing her hips and circling her arms above her head. She pored over the racks and held clothes up in front of the mirror, sucking in her cheeks. When she had finished with the garments, she let them fall to the floor like she was in a bric-a-brac market rather than Olive's room.

Olive made the spare bed. She then folded a towel, all fancy like a napkin, placed a bar of soap on top, and put it on Pip's bed. She'd seen this done at hotels with Mog and it looked very sophisticated and very welcoming. If Pip noticed, she didn't care, though, because she plonked herself down on top of it. 'So, you talk about Mog but what about WhatsisnameSeed?'

Olive picked up a leftover sheet and let the hem drop to the carpet.

'Where is he?'

Olive held the sheet out from her body and gathered the ends together, neatly drawing edge to edge. 'I don't know. Mog never mentions him. It's sort of a no-go area. Every time I try she just freezes up, so I don't. It's easier.'

Olive folded the sheet again and again until it was so thick it wouldn't bend. She held it to her nose, breathing in the clean smells of cotton and washing powder. It was hard to explain to people that she wouldn't even recognize her own father if he turned up to collect her from school.

'What does he do?' pressed Pip. She was leaning forwards on the spare bed, trying to catch Olive's eye.

'I don't know what he does, where he lives or whether he's even alive.' Olive stared at the faded flyspot pattern on the sheet. 'All I know is that he was a flaky hippy who was too liberal with his love.' She picked at a cotton thread trailing from the sheet's corner.

'That's not much to go on. There must be clues. Haven't you checked the mail? Maybe he sends cheques or Christmas cards or something?'

Olive shrugged. 'I don't think so. Mog wouldn't like that. I don't think he cares.'

'You're nuts. I bet he's gazing out at the night sky as we speak, wondering where his baby is, feeling happy that no matter what, he's under the same moon.'

'Babies.' Olive shook her head. 'That might freak him.'

Pip flipped her plaits over her shoulders and started swaying about the room. She threw her arms about theatrically, trying to reflect the gravitas of the situation (although she looked like Nut Allergy doing an impression of an elephant in Drama Dance). 'I bet he studies every girl and tries to work out how old she is and whether she could be his daughter. Maybe he has an entire room filled to the ceiling with letters addressed to you and stamped RETURN TO SENDER – and maybe he goes into his room every night and cries, wishing that he'd never been such a flaky hippy who was too liberal with his love.'

'I don't think so.' Olive gripped the cotton thread and tugged until it snapped. 'I'm twelve and he's never tried to contact me. Not once.'

Pip shrugged. The air in the room had somehow flattened, lost its zest. It had become solemn and grown up. Not grown up in an exuberant Mog way, but grown up in a severe discussion-about-bills, children-go-to-the-next-room, Grahams sort of way.

Olive took out a pair of pyjamas and handed them to Pip. Her mood had congealed. 'Come on,' she said, more primly than she'd intended. 'It's a school night. Let's get ready for bed.'

Olive sounded just like Mrs Graham.

11
Plankton or Krill

When the girls woke the next morning, Mog had already come and gone. In her wake was a trail of burnt toast crusts, laddered tights and documents. Pip picked up a folder tied in pink ribbon.

IN THE MATTER OF THE DPP V MISS SARAH MCNAMARA
BRIEF TO COUNSEL TO APPEAR IN THE SUPREME COURT
OF VICTORIA PREPARED FOR MS MOG GARNAUT QC
INSTRUCTING SOLICITORS FOR THE DEFENDANT,
GLICKFELD & SARATCHANDRAN

'Don't.' Olive tried to snatch the papers from Pip. 'They're Mog's, and she doesn't like anybody to touch them. Not even me. They're very important and very confidential.'

'Sorry.' Pip put them down, a darn sight more

carefully than she had put down Olive's clothes, Olive noted. Mog set very few rules for Olive, but the one thing she was picky about was her work.

While Pip slopped chocolate spread and peanut butter onto her toast, the kitchen bench and the floor, Olive tore around the house trying to cobble together two school uniforms. The uniforms they'd had on the day before were dirty, and Olive's school was very strict about presentation. In junior school the teachers had checked the girls' undies every day to ensure that they were regulation green, and sent very terse notes home to the parents when they weren't.

Uniforms sorted, Olive parted her hair in front of the bathroom mirror and bound it in two straight plaits, which hung like fish spines down her back. She carefully covered the elastics with green satin ribbons, then folded her ankle socks over twice so that the edges were neat.

Olive had put a spare uniform out on the bed for Pip, together with her old black party shoes. While they were dusty, they would have to do until she managed to fossick another pair for her sister – hopefully from lost property. Probably junior-school lost property. The patent leather party shoes were from Grade 5 and, although they were definitely not regulation, they still fitted. Olive had been medium height in Grade 4, smallish in Grade 5, tiny in Grade 6, and now, in Year 7, she was a bona fide midget.

'It's because she doesn't have a mother there to cook properly for her,' Mrs Graham had whispered to Mr Graham one night at Mathilda's, not quite softly enough. 'She eats like a bird.'

'Rubbish,' Mr Graham had replied. 'Mog Garnaut was a late bloomer. Olive'll grow, and if she grows into legs half as long as her mother's, the men of Greater Melbourne will be extremely grateful.'

Despite Mr Graham's support, Olive couldn't be so sure. She was the smallest girl in the entire senior school, other than the dwarf.

Olive smiled. 'The *equal* second smallest,' she corrected herself, remembering Pip.

Whatever happened at school, Olive was determined not to introduce Pip to Amelia. She didn't want Pip to wish for a moment that she was related to somebody taller or cooler, with a straighter parting or a beach house. Amelia already had Mathilda.

Thirty minutes later, as Olive caught sight of the school fence, the Till–Mill saga came tumbling back in gruesome detail.

'Pip,' Olive called to her sister. The girls were trudging uphill towards the school gates from the spot where the taxi had dropped them. Olive always asked taxis to drop her in the lane beside the school so that nobody would see her arrive. She'd much rather have come to school on the tram like normal girls, but to do this she'd have to leave home soon after six.

Pip was sulking because her school bag was heavy and she didn't see the point in walking any further than necessary. If Pip had her way, they'd probably have been driven to the classroom door. 'Who cares if people see?' she had muttered. 'They'll just be jealous that while they have to turn up in the family station wagon, we're like movie stars.' Olive had let her walk on ahead.

'Pip,' Olive called again. 'Wait!'

Pip paused until Olive caught up, and the twins walked on for a few more steps in silence. *Left, right, left*.

The morning light was so strong it was crackly. Olive took a deep breath. 'You know how there's a food chain in every school?'

Pip nodded and readjusted her bag.

'Well, Amelia – and probably Mathilda too now – are blue whales.'

Pip nodded.

'And I'm . . . well. Well, I'm plankton.'

Olive's heart fluttered while she waited for Pip's response. There wasn't one.

'Actually, if Nut Allergy's plankton,' continued Olive, 'I guess . . . I guess I'm more your average krill.'

Olive waited for Pip to dump her. She waited for Pip to say, 'On second thoughts, I'd rather not be your sister. In fact, I'd rather be anybody but Nut Allergy's sister, and if she's worked on her bladder control, I'll even choose her.' But she didn't. Pip shrugged and said, 'Whatever – I'm happy being krill.' Olive beamed. The wider her smile spread, the more she grew to accommodate it.

Pip stopped walking and spun round to face Olive. 'There's a kid in your class called *Nut Allergy*?'

'It's not her real name, but her mum made her wear a sign around her neck in Prep so the teachers didn't feed her peanut butter or anything. Apparently one tiny bit, one sniff even, and she swells up like Veruca Salt. The name sort of stuck.'

'So what's her real name?'

'Oh, something boring. I forget. She got her period in Grade Three, though.'

Pip kept walking and Olive bounded after her.

When Pip and Olive reached the wrought-iron gates, the school emblem with its curly scrolls and Latin writing glared down at them. Mog had once quipped that it was very appropriately shaped like a dollar sign.

'What does it mean?' asked Pip.

Olive couldn't even pronounce the school motto, let alone remember what it stood for. 'No idea. "Education, Ambition and Success for Women in Work" or something.' The bell had rung and the grounds were deserted. Olive walked faster.

'"Education, Ambition and Success for Women in Green Cotton Bog-catchers", more likely,' said Pip, whose green knickers must have been slurping up her bottom as she kept plucking them out. 'These undies are horri—' Pip stopped when she saw the schoolhouse.

The Joanne d'Arc School for Girls was certainly imposing. It was a huge Gothic building, which sat high on a hill and housed a teaching institution for the elite from Melbourne and the surrounding districts.

'Heck,' said Pip. 'This place looks like Hogwarts. Do you get to play Quidditch here, too?'

'I wish,' said Olive, thinking that she'd take her broomstick and burn right back home again, far and away from Till–Mill.

'Why are there bars on the windows?'

It wasn't an unreasonable question, but Olive had never noticed. She now wondered how she'd missed the thick metal rods that were welded to the front of each window frame. Olive shrugged. 'To make the boarders feel safe, I guess.'

The Joanne d'Arc boarders were girls who got to sleep at school in dorms and kick around on the play equipment at weekends. During the week they hung out in packs, ate pies and bonded over the knowledge that they had snuck their pyjamas in under their skirts. The boarders were special. They were always 'in', even when there was no doubt that as daygirls they'd have been 'out'. The rules were somehow different for boarders. They were one big happy gaggle of accepting sisters, arms firmly linked. Olive had been desperate to be a boarder – until she'd seen the state of the showers.

'They lock the boarders in?' Pip looked horrified. 'What did they do wrong?' The romance of boarding was lost on Pip. She muttered about the inhumanity of imprisoning people all the way to the classroom.

Year 7C was deep in the throes of origami when Olive and Pip arrived. Mrs Kato, Olive's Japanese teacher, smiled tightly from under her bun as they entered.

Olive wasn't fooled. Mrs Kato may have looked demure, but she was an inner knuckle-caner.

'Tardiness is the height of rudeness,' she said at least once a week. 'In Japan, it shows that you have very little respect for the company you are keeping. It can cost you your reputation and your friendships.'

'*Kato Sensei, ohayoo gozaimasu.*' Olive bowed her head. 'Um, sorry. This i—'

'*Suwatte kudasai,*' said Mrs Kato, gesturing to Olive's seat. Olive bit her lip and sat down. Pip slid into the empty desk beside her. Mrs Kato brought over a couple of pieces of red paper with a clover print, and the girls started to make paper cranes too.

'What crap,' said Pip. Origami required neat lines and precision. Pip's crane was looking more like a fish-and-chip wrapper – all grubby and over-fingered.

Olive swivelled round. Directly behind Pip, Amelia was folding her paper carefully, whispering to Mathilda. Her yellow-blonde hair with its perfect north–south parting gleamed in the sun that streamed through the window, and her honey tan cast a warm glow onto her desk.

'Till, I *can't* believe I forgot to tell you. Did you hear my cousin Poppy was hospitalized last night? She ate chilli because she wanted to make her lips big – sort of like collagen – and they nearly exploded.' Amelia lived in a world in which there was always a crisis.

Olive went to turn back to her origami, but Mathilda caught her eye. 'Why were you late?' she asked.

'Probably caught up doing a spot of early morning metal-detecting,' said Amelia. 'I know I find it hard to pull myself away.' They both laughed.

Pip looked at Olive and raised an eyebrow in a question mark. Olive drew two big arrows on the back of her exercise book. One was marked *Amelia*, the other *Mathilda*. Pip spun round and stared. '*That's* Amelia?'

Olive nodded.

'Ooooh, she's so brown. Especially her teeth.' Pip's mouth was pulled up on the side in a sort of snarl. 'Hey, baby Barbie. Chilli-lips are *not* a calamity. Your world's tinier than a Tic Tac.'

'Pip! Shush!' Olive sniggered and looked round. She had never heard a single girl sing anything other than Amelia's praise. Neither had Amelia.

Amelia's face had gone pale under her tan and her mouth had dropped open. Her hand shot up her side, as straight as a flagpole, waving Mrs Kato over.

'What's that? Some sort of Hitler Youth salute?' hissed Pip.

'Mrs Kato! Mrs Kato! Olive Garnaut is being *extremely* rude,' said Amelia, doing her best World Vision look: wide-eyed, and up through her lashes. 'Can you please ask her to move?' Now Olive's mouth dropped open. 'I didn't say—'

'*Shizuka ni shite kudasai!*' snapped Mrs Kato, and the class hum deadened. 'Olive Garnaut, you have been warned. Class, open your exercise books to page thirty-four and commence practising the kanji characters for the seasons. These are to be submitted to me by recess.'

Olive felt a blush creep up her neck. Just the thought of a blush made her blush more. She looked over at her sister and glared. Pip looked straight ahead.

12
Origami Massacre

Even before the class broke for recess, it was official. Olive Garnaut had an enemy. Previously she had been nothing but a low-grade irritant to Amelia, but Amelia, clearly realizing her pride was at stake, returned Pip's insult with a bomb.

'I'm going to get you, Olive Garnaut,' she said, loud enough for Olive and Pip to hear (but not Mrs Kato). She kicked at Olive's chair. Olive was working on the character for autumn, and her calligraphy pen shot up, making a thick black scar across her page.

Amelia leaned right forward over Olive's shoulder. 'You're such a dog, Olive Got-no-noughts, that your father took one look at you and bolted, and your mother hates you so much that, from what I hear, she can't stand hanging around either.'

'Amelia.' Mathilda giggled quietly.

Olive gripped her pen so hard her fingers were white where they pressed. She kept her eyes on the desk and tore the ruined page from her book.

'At least Mog is making something of herself, something important. Something other than muffins,' Pip spat back.

The bell rang. The class scattered and most of the girls streamed outside. Amelia and Mathilda flowed out with them.

'They're awful. I can't believe you were ever friends with them. They make me so angry, I just want to . . .' Pip punched the air with her puny arm. She looked so silly that both girls laughed. They sat together in silence.

'Do you think "dog" is maybe a nice term?' asked Olive. 'You know, cute like a puppy?' The desk clicked as Olive's legs swung under it.

'Sure,' said Pip in a tone that was kind but meant *I very much doubt it*.

Pip sucked her plait. Olive stared at a corner of the desk. The clicking slowed.

'Do you think he did do that? You know . . .' Olive paused. She picked at a strip of linoleum that was lifting from the side of the desk.

'Bolt?' Pip asked carefully through her plait. 'I don't know.' She sucked harder, as if trying to extract the answer. 'But I do think we have to find out more about this Custard Seed.'

'Mustard, not Custard.' Olive almost smiled.

'Ah, Custard, Mustard, I bet he's tidy.' Pip looked at the parallel lines of pencils on Olive's desk. 'And probably good at origami. Judging by Mog's bedroom, I don't suppose she's a natural at cranes, either.'

Olive dipped her head in a half-nod.

'I bet he's kind and funny with twinkly eyes and whiskers that tickle when he gives hugs.' Visions of Mustard Seed animated Pip's face.

Olive smiled. 'When I was little I always imagined that he chopped wood and that he had a tummy slung over his belt.'

Pip jumped out of the chair. 'I bet he has scruffy boat shoes that are so worn down if I hopped in them, I'd walk like he does.' Pip lolloped about the room with a wide-legged stride.

Olive laughed. The tempo of the desk-clicking increased as her legs swung faster. 'Boat shoes? Do you think he's a sailor?'

'Look, I have no idea whether he's a lawyer, a lock-smith or a lobster-catcher, but we need clues, and Mog's the only one who's got them. I think we should ask her.'

Olive turned back to her work.

'So, can we?'

Olive trailed the calligraphy pen up and across her page, concentrating on relaxing her shoulders, trying to let the ink glide, run free, as Mrs Kato insisted they should. 'Well, I guess I could try tonight.'

Olive felt Pip's smile before she saw it. Pip hooted. 'I'll start writing a list of questions.'

'But only if Mog's not too tired,' said Olive, horrified.

'Sure.' Pip swung her plait back over her shoulder. 'I'm starving, by the way.'

Olive pointed Pip in the direction of the cheesy rolls at the tuckshop. They were bright orange and the melted cheese was so perfectly cooked that you could pull it into strings a metre long. 'Make sure you push,' Olive called after Pip. 'That tuckshop can be a jungle.'

'Olive-*san*? How are your characters progressing?' Mrs Kato was at the front of the room doing remedial work with Nut Allergy, who was humped over the desk. Lim May Yee and a couple of other boarders were comparing chocolate crackles down the back.

'I'm nearly done.' Olive went back to her calligraphy. She became so completely absorbed by the curving lines and flickering images of WilliamPetersMustardSeed that she didn't hear anyone approaching.

WilliamPetersMustardSeed *did* think of her – Pip had to be right. Olive thought of him, and had thought of him for as long as she could remember. Even when she was doing something else, he was always there: a bit of him just sort of hung around, standing stage-left of her thoughts. It made sense that he would also —

Snip.

Olive started when she heard the crisp metallic slice. She felt a breeze on the back of her neck. Before she could register what had happened, one of her fish-spine plaits lay across her lap. Puny and white-blonde, it curled up at the end like baby hair. Her hair. Her hair like Mog's. Her hair like Pip's.

The room was silent. The chocolate-crackle girls had stopped comparing. They looked at Olive and then at Mathilda, who was brandishing a pair of scissors.

Mathilda looked at Amelia, standing beside her.

'My teeth are *not* brown,' said Amelia.

Olive yelped. The chocolate-crackle girls yelped. Mrs Kato, who had been packing up her class materials, saw Olive's lopsided hair and yelped. 'Mathilda Graham, this is quite intolerable. You will come with me to see Mrs Dalling *ima*.'

'Amelia made me —'

'*Ima*,' barked Mrs Kato.

Mathilda was marched out of the door by Mrs Kato, in the full knowledge that she would probably be marched out of the Joanne d'Arc School for Girls.

Amelia turned her nose up to the sky, pirouetted, and walked out behind them.

It was a short battle. The stakes were high, but in her own wonky-haired way, Olive had won; well, at least she wasn't in the headmistress's office. There was no getting around it, though: her plait was a clear loser.

Pip, returning from the tuckshop, stopped in the doorway. 'Oh, Ol, what has she done?' She raced over to her one-plaited sister and stroked the stumpy knob of hair that spiked out from its elastic. 'That bully.'

'It was *Mathilda*,' said Olive, showing the first signs of recovering from shock. 'Mathilda did it?' Olive posed the last statement as a question. She was confused. Big tears streamed down her face, joining tributaries of watery mucus.

'Mathilda? That pig is so spineless. I have no doubt that Amelia was behind it, though. I hope they're both throttled for this. In fact, I hope they're both re-incarnated as weevils.'

Olive shook her head and sniffed.

Pip sat back. 'It's very modern,' she said. 'A bit sort of punk.' She stroked Olive's head.

'I don't want modern hair.' Olive started to weep again. 'I don't even like uneven hems.'

News about the slaughter had shot outside the classroom and around the school. Year 7s were very efficient conductors of information. Girls stood at the door of the classroom, holding back but peering forward, trying to catch a glimpse of Olive and her plait stump – like pedestrians at a car crash.

'You could bob it,' said Lim May Yee, coming over. 'I think your hair would look great bobbed.'

'I agree. I think your hair will look much better bobbed. I was thinking of doing it to mine, too.' Pip handed Olive a piece of origami paper. 'Here, blow your nose.'

Olive blew her nose all over Pip's crane.

'My cousin says that hair carries memories,' said Lim May Yee.

'Then I guess that half of mine have just been butchered.' Olive pulled gently on her blunt plait-tuft.

'Let's hope it's the half with Mathilda and Amelia.'

Olive managed to smile. Lim May Yee handed her a sweet. It was chewy but spicy. 'Indonesian ginger. Mum sends them from home.'

'It's delicious,' said Olive. 'Thanks, Lim May Yee.'

'My pleasure.' She paused. 'You can just call me May, by the way. That's actually my name. My surname's Lim, and in my culture, because family is the most important thing, the Lim bit goes first. That's all.'

'Oh,' said Olive, chewing. 'Were you born in May?'

'Nope. September. And if you think that's weird, my sister's called Sunday and she was born on a Thursday.'

Olive laughed. May smiled and walked back to the boarders.

'She's nice,' said Pip. 'A bit bow-legged, but funny.'

'No memories.' Olive twirled her remaining plait around her finger. 'It's probably not a bad time for a fresh start.'

'There's no doubt,' said Pip. 'Those old memories were starting to wilt like carrots left too long in the crisper.'

13
Bury Him

Olive sat in front of the mirror while Pip attempted to even out her hair. The second plait lay on the kitchen table like a dead animal. Olive watched as her sister waved the scissors around her face. 'Pip, concentrate! It's not straight!'

'First I putta da towel, then I cutta da hair.' Pip was doing a lousy impersonation of Pirelli from *Sweeney Todd* and it was making Olive edgy. For a girl who was so condescending about *The Little Mermaid*, Pip had managed to work an awful lot of musicals into her repertoire.

'Pip, please! Careful! Here, give me the scissors – I'll do it.'

'Olive, you are such a worrywart. It only has to get you through until tomorrow.'

'Well I don't want to look like a freak.'

'You don't want to look like everybody else, anyway –

not with a name like Olive.'

'Olive's not that weird.'

'No, but you're the only one in the school.'

That was true. 'Whenever I complain about my name, Mog says that when I was born, there were seven other babies in the house – three called Sunny, three called Rainbow and one boy called Rani. Poor Rani really lucked out. His name means Indian princess.'

The girls laughed, and the scissors veered north. Pip looked at Olive's face. 'I've got to go,' she said and scuttled out of the room.

After Pip had left, Olive ran a brush through her hair. It jolted when it came to the ends and she combed the air. Short hair was going to take a bit of getting used to. Olive flattened her bob and examined the cut. It was a teensy bit longer on the left than the right, but it would do until she went to the hairdresser.

Mrs Graham had booked Olive in. She had been so appalled by Mathilda's behaviour that she had rung Mog at work that afternoon to apologize. Then Amelia's mother had rung Mog to apologize, too. Well, sort of apologize.

'We are obviously very upset, but furious that the school has let things disintegrate to this level. This is not the Joanne d'Arc School for Girls that I know. They have suspended Mathilda Graham for one day and given both girls two Saturday detentions. While Mathilda is clearly a very bad influence on Amelia, Luke and I were not certain that Joanne d'Arc was right for our daughter anyway, and we have been investigating other possibilities.

It must be said, strictly off the record, that the facilities at Paronton are now infinitely superior.'

'Strictly off the record,' Mog had replied, trying to reformat a document.

'But it is a difficult choice,' Amelia's mother had continued, 'and not one we take lightly. We've got three generations of Joanne d'Arc girls in this family. You weren't at Joanne d'Arc. Where were you? They certainly didn't have that terrible outdoor programme when I was in Year Nine. One term in the bush – no phones, no electricity. Dreadful. How will Amelia blow-dry her hair?'

'Three generations! No hairdryers!' Mog had laughed later on the phone to Olive.

Mog was still laughing when she walked into the kitchen. Olive glanced at Pip, who had been using her bare feet and hands to shimmy up the doorframe for the past hour. Pip started giggling too.

'So is Amelia leaving school?' Olive leaned forward to give Mog a kiss hello and Mog sat down next to her.

'No. Liz Forster went through all that laborious detail to tell me that "on balance" they've "decided against a transfer". On balance?! I bet she's the kind of woman who irons tea towels.'

'She is!' laughed Olive. 'She has them ironed. And underpants.'

'Oh dear.' Mog shook her head and smiled. 'She really is the pits.' Mog stroked Olive's freshly cropped hair.

'Do I look like a freak?' Olive nuzzled against Mog's

shoulder like she used to when she was a baby.

'Olive Garnaut, no! You do not look like a freak!'
Olive could smell smoke and toothpaste on Mog's breath.
'But you do look exactly like your mother.'

'Exactly?' Olive pushed her head further into Mog's
arm. Mog was trying to flick through the post over
Olive's shoulder.

'Exactly. I'll try to dig you up an old school photo of
mine.' Mog looked down at Olive's face. 'Is that such a
bad thing?'

'No. But don't I look even a tiny bit like . . .
WilliamPetersMustardSeed?' Olive mouthed his name
with her lips.

'Like whom?' Mog peered under the edge of an
envelope. Olive took a deep breath.

'Like WilliamPetersMustardSeed.'

Olive held her breath. Pip had said it, really said it.
His name stained the air.

Mog's lipstick-smile dropped. She stopped flicking.
Pip was still. Mog exhaled, and her shoulders dropped
down after her smile. She held Olive out from her chest.
'You know I don't like that name in this house, Olive. We
have no secrets here, but trust me, this is important.'

'But why don't I see him? Ingrid, Louisa and Lisa all
have divorced parents and they see their dads every
second weekend and go to the football and the zoo and
get show bags. And Melody Moore lives with her
dad.'

Mog raised her eyebrow in the manner she usually
reserved for ladies in city department stores and

barristers on the Other Side. 'Don't whinge, Olive.'

Olive's top lip quivered.

Mog softened and pulled her daughter back towards her. 'He's not a father, Ol. He hasn't acted like a father, now or ever. We lived a very different type of life down the coast to the one that we live now.'

Pip's eyebrows shot up.

'Which coast?'

'You are trying! The Victorian coast. I don't expect you to understand, but things were different. We squatted. That means we didn't pay rent. It was illegal, but we didn't care. But now I'm an officer of the law – I enforce the law. Those days were OK, in part, but they could work against me, especially for my chances of getting on the Bench, and we don't want anything to jeopardize that. I've worked too hard, and I have enough against me already.'

Olive nodded. The Bench and sitting on it was all Mog wanted. Olive knew that 'certain people' were conservative, and that 'certain people' looked down on single mothers, even if those single mothers were like Mog and darn good at their jobs.

'Although, if William's still there, he's probably got a good case for adverse possession.' Mog laughed.

'What's adverse possession?' Olive was relieved that Mog's mood had passed.

'It means that you inhabit a property for such a long period of time that it becomes yours. Like those people in the Clare Renner library. They squatted in the basement with padlocks for so many years that the Council had to pass them the title papers. They stayed put. But really, Ol, forget it all. It's easier to sit on these things, bury them.'

'Bury what? I don't even know what he does.' Olive picked at a piece of fluff through a cigarette burn in the sofa arm.

'Olive, please don't pick. I left William and went back to law because I realized that I deserved better; that *we* deserved much better. Our life is good. You have an excellent role model and everything you possibly need. Now please, can we forget him? He wasn't worth the angst then and he certainly isn't worth it now. The only decent thing he did in his entire life was produce – no, rather, contribute to the production of – you.' Mog kissed Olive's soft blonde down. 'And that is priceless.'

Mog went back to the post. Olive slipped out of her chair and went to join Pip. They headed to Olive's room and closed the door.

'Man, I see what you mean. She may have been trying to *look* calm, but she was so worked up, her neck was stringy.' Pip's face was flushed and her eyes shone.

'She's OK,' said Olive. 'She does a good job. We get by.'

'But we didn't get many clues.'

'I think we should forget it, Pip. It's not worth making Mog angry.'

'Forget it? Are you mad? We know this much.' Pip took out a notebook and started to write.

CLUES
WilliamPetersMustardSeed

Coast – Victoria
Adverse possession
Possibly likes mustard
Not worth it

'There must be something else,' said Pip. 'Clothing? Letters?'

'I swear, there's nothing. It's like he never existed. She's deleted him, and I want to, too.'

Pip stared at her.

'Can you just leave it? It doesn't seem right.' Olive ripped the clue list out of the notebook.

'Sure.' Pip glared at Olive and left the room.

14
History-shuffle

Olive stalked to the kitchen and pulled out her paints. She liked to paint whenever she felt tight, and she felt tight now. Even the smell of the watercolour, the thickness of the paper, was enough to calm her. Olive ran the bristles of a brush along her fingers. It may have been bad for the fibres, but Olive loved the way the tips felt like cats' tails (without the fleas).

Mog was in her study working. Every so often, Olive could hear her turn the page of a document. Pip's whereabouts was anyone's guess. Olive sat at the kitchen table and painted until the hard wood of the chair made her legs prickle.

As much as Olive wanted to delete WilliamPeters-MustardSeed, she couldn't. It was a funny thing, to imagine a father. Her missing father wasn't like a missing person, because there was no photograph. He was more like the chalk outline of a body on the pavement in a New York murder; a gap Olive needed to fill, but whose insides were still unknown. A gap that could perhaps only be coloured in by reference to Mog. But it was unclear if Mog and Mustard Seed were like skinny Jack Sprat who ate no fat and his wife who ate no lean, or if they were both, in fact, Jack Sprats.

From the pieces she had, Olive couldn't picture whether he was a noisy honker of a man who would have been banned from attending netball matches for overzealous parental support, or whether he was a barrel-chested partygoer in an open shirt, telling stories with a glass of red wine. Maybe he was the sort of person to talk loudly about shares on his mobile phone in public places. 'Sell, sell, sell.'

It was always possible that he wore a navy fisherman's cap, walked a Westie and smelled of rum and tuna, with scars on his hands from oyster shells – or perhaps he was more like the personal trainers who urged panting women around the park: 'I've got clients twice your age who could run rings around you.' He could have resembled the school gardener, a man with dirt that would never wash out of the lines in his palms and manure scraped up the back of his overalls. Or perhaps he was like Hugh Jackman (the only actor Mog had ever declared *very handsome*), or a crier like Prince Frederick at the Danish Royal Wedding.

Whenever Olive noticed a man on the street or in the newspaper, she added him to her mental catalogue of possible Mustard Seeds, until he managed to be a jumble of everything: a netball-supporting gardener who drank wine, traded stocks over his mobile, danced, and cried in Danish.

A while later – when her glass of painting water had turned the colour of a grape milkshake – Olive's quiet was interrupted.

'Olive, c'mon, where are the photos? There must be some and I can't find them anywhere.'

Olive moaned. Pip was as persistent as a terrier. 'There's only a very old album with photos of me and Mog. He's not there, Pip. I know because I've checked a trillion times.'

Pip, however, promised that she would leave Olive to paint in peace if Olive indulged her this one time.

Olive snuck past the study. The door was open and it was chaotic. Mog's desk featured an in-tray for documents she had yet to get to, and an out-tray for documents that she had completed. The trays were piled with cigarette lighters, wads of unpaid bills and orphaned high heels, but Mog said they gave her the impression that she had a system; that she could be organized if she wanted to be. And that, Mog said, was important.

Mog was stooped over a document with her chin tucked into her neck. Just seeing Mog hunched like that made Olive stand tall. She dragged the album up from under the coffee table in the lounge and headed towards her room.

'Ol?' There was a thud as a pile of Mog's books rolled backwards off her desk. 'Bugger! Olive?'

Olive froze. She could see Mog through the open door. The album was too big to hide behind her back, so she dropped it and stood on it. Her heart thrashed against her ribs. Mog stopped reading and looked up, an unlit cigarette poised between her first two fingers, which were held in an elegant V for victory (appropriate as she always won her cases). 'Ol, can you grab me a lighter?' Mog took off her glasses and rubbed the crease between her eyebrows. 'I'd also kill for a coffee.' Olive watched as Mog's fingernail tapped the desk. It was long and nicotine-yellow.

'Sure,' said Olive, so relieved that she forgot to reprimand Mog for the minutes of her life that she was puffing away.

Olive left the album on the floor and headed to the kitchen. When she returned, Mog was unloading bundles of briefs tied with hot-pink ribbon. 'I almost forgot to tell you. I met a parent of a friend of yours yesterday.'

'You did?' Olive was confused. So far as she knew, she didn't have any friends except Pip, who was family and didn't count.

'He's the instructing solicitor on this case. Smith, Jason Smith. Nice man. Earnest but smart – his two girls are at Joanne d'Arc. Kate's in your year and Melanie's a few years behind. He said that you and Kate sometimes have lunch together.'

'We do? Kate who?' asked Olive, making a mental note to hunt the mysterious Kate down should Pip ever take ill or end up at school camp at a different time.

'Kate Smith, I assume. Unless the girls are under their mum's name. She's a solicitor as well.'

'Oh, must be.' Olive had no idea who Mog was talking about.

Olive picked the album off the ground and headed back to her bedroom. Pip grabbed it from her and pored over the photos. 'I know there'll be more clues in here. Hey, check this one out. Mog's a classic.' Mog was lying back on a beanbag, wearing a tie-dyed T-shirt that said I KISSED A FAIRY AT PORT FAIRY FOLK FESTIVAL. 'Fairy festival? What's that?' Pip laughed. 'You think she wore fairy wings?'

'Shush, Mog'll kill us if she finds us,' Olive whispered. There really were two types of people, she thought. Olive was quiet. She liked to make herself thin; to creep through life. Pip, however, was loud. Everything she did was noisy, even the way she chewed apples (like a horse) and walked (slapping her feet like a seal). Mog was a combo. She was noisy but she hated talk at certain times, like when she had a hangover. She always said that the worst things in the morning were eggs and noise. After 10 a.m., however, Mog was a foghorn.

Once Pip had gone through all the photos, they added the following to the list:

Tie-dye
Port Fairy Folk Festival
Yoga
Vegetable patch

'Study the backgrounds. There must be something else.' Pip bent back down over the album.

Olive, who had now well and truly abandoned any idea of painting, turned the page to a photo of Mog and a baby in a vegetable patch. There were a number of photos of Mog in shorts and a bikini top pulling weeds in this vegetable patch, her face and back speckled by the sun. 'Hey, check this out!' said Olive, her voice high. 'You're there, too.'

'What?' Pip looked up from her list. 'No way, shut up, get out of here.' But Olive was right. There was Mog in the vegetable patch holding not one but two pale babies wrapped in saffron robes.

'How did *that* happen?' Olive's voice was not only high, it was also squeaky. 'I've seen that photo a thousand times before.'

'I don't know, but we've got our clue.'

'How can you think of clues at a time like this?' Olive looked down at the photo again.

'Look!'

Suddenly, Olive knew exactly what Pip was talking about and wondered how she had ever missed it. The lighthouse, the lighthouse. Mog was standing in a long vegetable patch. Just behind the garden was a lighthouse. It was not a tall lighthouse, as far as Olive could see, but it was a pretty one. It was quite squat, with a thick base of limestone that resembled lumps of sugar. The top was off-white and peeling. Both the garden and lighthouse were encircled by a picket fence with missing posts, like forgotten items on a shopping list.

'What's that thing?' Pip pointed at a dot where the lighthouse's peak met the sky. Olive grabbed the magnifying glass she had used to burn ants in J-school. Under the magnifying glass, Olive could see that at the top of the lighthouse was a tiny window, like an eye – only the glass was broken. A purple sheath of fabric – cloth or a towel, perhaps – flapped from it.

'I don't know,' said Olive. 'But if this lighthouse is flying flags and the window is broken, I don't think it works.'

'You're a genius, Holmes.' Pip added the final and best clue to the list.

Abandoned lighthouse (limestone base)

'I'm still freaked out about you being in that photo.' Olive pushed her finger down on the two babies in their saffron robes. The cellophane crackled.

Pip shrugged. 'Forget the photo. It makes sense that history shuffled a bit to make room for me. It would be kind of hurtful if it didn't.'

Olive rolled her eyes.

'The important thing is that WilliamPetersMustard-Seed is one step closer.' Pip beat the biro down on the page. 'Now, we just need to do some careful research.'

Mog coughed in the next room. Her cough was deep and rattly.

'We can't use the computer tonight.' Olive gestured towards Mog's study. 'Anyway, I hope you're better at research than you are at origami, or we won't find him until we're grown up with our own kids.'

Pip snapped the album shut. 'Plenty of world leaders were hopeless at cranes, Olive. Do you think Margaret Thatcher knew how to fold a crane?'

Olive tried to remember who Margaret Thatcher was exactly.

'Well I doubt it, Olive Garnaut. Margaret Thatcher was Prime Minister of England, and she was much too busy learning important stuff like law and politics, and how to sip tea without getting lipstick on the cup.' And with that, Pip stood and marched out of the room.

15
Yellow Peril

The following morning, Pip was grumpy. As expected, Mog had hogged the Internet the night before, and Olive did not need *in-tu-ition* to tell that the wait to begin research was killing her sister. Pip had done every celebrity crossword in Mog's magazines and repeatedly checked whether the study light was still on, but Mog was on an all-nighter for the Big Case and couldn't be stopped.

'Doesn't she ever sleep?'

'She'll do three or four nights straight and then crash for twenty hours at the end,' said Olive.

'Well, I'm not waiting for the weekend before I start.'

'Pip, don't worry about it. Mog might be at it again tonight, but the computer should be free sometime over the weekend. And we can always try the library.'

Pip's mood deteriorated further at school, as the library server had crashed. Luckily house meetings had been convened to replace the daily hymn-singing, prayer-spouting assembly.

The school was divided into four 'houses', represented by four colours: red (Turner), blue (Wilkinson), green (Grieves) and yellow (Burnett). The houses were named to honour previous headmistresses and teachers who would otherwise have sunk into grim obscurity.

Mr Hollywood – who taught Maths and was every bit as theatrical as his name suggested – said that nowadays teachers got nothing but Task Assessments and After-Hours Marking. He was lobbying for a fifth house named 'Hollywood' (which would clearly have to be pink). Olive didn't like his chances, though. A local school supplies company wanted naming rights in exchange for an annual donation.

Mathilda was in Wilkinson (soon to be *Foley's Quality School Supplies* Wilkinson). Olive was in Burnett, and so was Amelia.

Olive and Pip walked into the old ballroom that doubled as Burnett's homeroom. Around them, colossal girls buzzed in blazers with yellow braid. Olive kept her eyes focused on the balling carpet, partly because she was self-conscious about her wonky hair, partly because she didn't want to see Amelia, and partly because she didn't want the big girls to remember that she hadn't returned her money for the chocolate drive.

She couldn't help but notice Amelia walking in front of her, though – a valley between the blazered giants.

She guided Pip to the left to give Amelia a very wide berth.

Olive had been at the school since kindergarten, but she didn't really have any friends in Burnett, and the tall girls made her feel nervous. In the first few weeks of the year, way before the whole Till–Mill saga, Olive and Amelia had sat near each other for these meetings: not quite next to, but near. While they didn't talk, it was a kind of Year 7 solidarity thing, when there was nobody better around.

Amelia knew lots of Burnett girls now, and she also seemed to be related to a good portion of them. Whenever they had Sports Day or the Swimming Carnival, Mrs Forster let Amelia bring in the hand-stitched Burnett banner that Amelia's grandmother had sewn as a girl. The banner was made with gold embroidery thread on merino wool, and Amelia draped it over her shoulders like a royal cloak.

The banner bestowed heritage – Amelia was practically a Burnett Aborigine (who hadn't been stripped of her rights). It didn't need to be said that her name would be embossed on the mahogany board for house captains, come Year 12. It would just be there, along with her mother's and her grandmother's; this was as much a fact as the collective straightness of the Forster women's teeth.

'So how did you end up in Burnett?' asked Pip as they claimed a couple of carpet squares in a poky corner of the room. It must have been clear to her that Olive had no friends and no Family Connection.

'I liked the colour.' Olive paused. What was not to like about yellow? 'I actually had no choice; it was allocated in Prep. But it's a good colour – the colour of everything happy and summery: sun, sand, mangoes, chicks—'

'Wee.'

It was true. Indian yellow paint was made with distilled cows' urine. Olive had read it once. They boiled it down into sticky goo before packaging it for painting. 'Thanks, Pip.' Olive looked at her sister. 'You always put such a gross spin on things.'

'Well, it's hardly the colour of everything happy.' Pip paused and gestured at Amelia, who was chatting to her Year 9 cousin, Poppy Atkinson, a bit further along the room. Poppy was leaning in towards Amelia with her hand near her mouth as a shield. They kept glancing in Olive's direction.

Pip directed a spaz-face at Poppy. 'That whole family looks yellow.'

'Pip, if you're going to say these things, can you at least say them quietly?'

'They do. All that fake-tan skin and peroxide: they're the modern yellow peril.'

'OK, girls, OK.' The house captain, Marie-Claire Coombs, was waving her arms at the front of the room, trying to get some quiet. Olive shook her head at Pip and leaned forwards to listen.

Although they made her nervous, Olive found the big girls glorious. There was an elegance to them, despite their height. No braces, no spots, no puffy faces. They wore beautiful dresses to the school dance and had their make-up done at Mecca. Olive would pore over their dance photos in the school magazine each Christmas: it was just like Joanne d'Arc's very own Oscars. Last year, they had even entered on a red carpet.

Marie-Claire Coombs may have been looking splendid, but she was also looking most disapproving. She put her hands on her hips. 'I have a list of girls who have not returned their money for the chocolate drive. As you know, this money was due in last week, and as a consequence of these few girls, Burnett is sitting third, not second, on the league tables. I personally feel really angry that the selfish acts of a thoughtless few have penalized us all in this way.'

There was a murmur around the room, a stirring, as if it were the speech given by William Wilberforce to abolish slavery. Hundreds of girls shook their heads in agreement with Marie-Claire Coombs and looked as if they would have said 'Hear-hear' had they been fat men in parliament.

Olive felt herself blush deep, deep crimson. She stared at a patch of carpet. How had Mog managed to forget for the second term in a row?

Nicole Reid, the vice-captain, handed Marie-Claire Coombs a list.

'Now, I have spoken to Nicole and we have decided to ask these girls, these Traitors of Burnett, to stand up at the end of this session when I call their names.'

'Oh, man,' said Olive. This was unbearable. What was Marie-Claire Coombs thinking? Olive didn't want to be lynched. The betrayal felt personal.

'Blashnarshoknnggfasdejdcdmeddmdsoedcjndecm.'

A gentle rolling of syllables tumbled over Olive. The syllables formed words that had no meaning; it sounded as if somebody was just speaking what they'd typed by sitting on a computer keyboard.

'Bihsogedjflofslkanfebhfqbecqejhifchokcvboqvhe-jkqbvejquchebihjcbebhmodi.'

'It's May,' whispered Pip.

'What?'

'Look – under there.'

Olive turned. Right against the wall, under a pile of pushed-back desks and chair-stacks, was a girl hunched over crossed legs, holding her hands to her ears and muttering.

'That's May?'

May heard her name and waved them over.

'Hang on. I'll wait here for you to be called,' said Pip.

'I'll be quick.' Olive crawled through the metal desk legs. 'Um, hi,' she whispered. 'What are you doing?'

'Trying to block them out,' May whispered back.

'Why?'

'I'm desperate. I can't believe it. I've done it again.' May shook her head.

'Done what?' Olive asked. May was pretty strange.

'Eaten the entire packet. Every single bar. I just can't believe it – it happens every year. I always mean to sell the chocolates, and I always eat them, even if they taste soapy and I can buy them for two dollars less at the milk bar.'

Olive nodded. 'Me too.'

'One of the Year Twelves says it's like a chocolate credit card. Eat first and worry about remembering the cash later.' May shook her head. 'Though all is not lost. I've had an idea.'

Olive could hear the drone of Nicole Reid's housekeeping above them. 'Hey, we should probably get back out there. They're getting us to stand up if we haven't handed in our money.'

'They're what?' May sat up so quickly she knocked her head on the roof of a desk.

'Marie-Claire Coombs wants us to stand if we haven't handed in our money.'

'This place is ruthless.' May rubbed her forehead. 'Marie-Claire Coombs spent too long on Duke of Ed hikes in her formative years.' She gave a very deep sigh and started crawling out behind Olive.

As the girls emerged, the floor echoed with the press of footsteps as Burnett stood to sing the cheer.

> *I don't know but I've been told*
> *Burnett Girls are Out for Gold*
> *Sound Off Sound Off*
> *Burrr-neeettt Burrr-neeettt*
> *Can we do it? Can we do it?*
> *Yes we* clap *sure can.*

Burnett finished with a few high whoops and a sprinkle of applause. Olive whooped and applauded just behind the pack. May didn't bother.

'It's lucky we're selling chocolate bars and not heading

off to war. That was terrible.' May frowned, sitting back down.

Olive nodded. 'If Joan of Arc had received that on her send-off she'd never have mounted the horse. She'd have got right back into her nightie and hopped into bed.'

The girls laughed.

At the front of the room, Marie-Claire Coombs shook a piece of paper. 'Right, that's enough. Could the following girls stand when I call their names. Starting in Year Seven . . .'

Olive wriggled. She leaned in towards Pip and May, her head down.

'. . . Vanessa Johnston, Alice Martin, Isabella Whitlam, Olive Garnaut and Lim May Yee.'

Olive stood. She stared at a piece of squashed chewing gum, smooth and grey on the ballroom floor.

Marie-Claire Coombs glared down along her bosom and the top of the list.

'I didn't forget mine,' said May.

Olive looked up. May looked pink. Marie-Claire Coombs looked surprised. 'This isn't really a forum for excuses.'

'I know, but it's not an excuse. I put my box on eBay and the auction doesn't close until the end of the weekend. It was already at forty-two dollars this morning, though. With any luck, I'll be able to trade them for another boarding house – like that American man who traded a paperclip for a house on the Internet.'

There was a twittering around the room. One of the boarders was laughing so hard, she started hiccuping.

'I see,' said Marie-Claire Coombs. 'Well, make sure you get a cheque to me on Monday. And in Year Eight, Eliza . . .'

Olive and May sat back down with a thump. Olive breathed out loudly. A boarder behind May poked her shoulder. 'Classic.'

'Thanks,' said May and turned to speak to her. 'Luckily you can buy those chocolates at any milk bar. I ate the lot.'

Pip smiled. 'She really is nuts.'

Ten minutes later, the bell rang for first period. Pip and Olive trailed along with the other Burnett girls until they were sucked out through the ballroom door. Year groups blended in the press.

Outside in the grey morning, Olive found herself behind Amelia. Amelia was still talking to Poppy Atkinson.

'So when will you know what's happening with Mary?' asked Poppy.

Pip raised an eyebrow. Everybody knew Amelia was meant to be Mary in the Christmas concert, despite the fact she was only in Year 7. Everybody also knew that she might be demoted because of the scissor incident.

'I have to go and see Mrs Dalling about it today. I'll be so furious if I lose it – it was *not* my fault.' Amelia looked round and caught Olive's eye. She threw Olive a very dirty look.

Poppy paused to pull up her sock. 'I wouldn't worry.

You're still the best actor in the school and besides, you weren't actually *holding* the scissors.'

Pip took Olive's arm. 'If I were the headmistress, I'd never let her act again.' She laughed. 'Well, not unless I needed somebody to play a tandoori chicken.'

Olive smiled, but only a bit, and watched Amelia walk off towards the middle-school piazza. She looked at the fresh new-white of Amelia's socks against her brown calves. She looked at Amelia's uniform, which she wore longer than most girls, with the belt looped twice around her hips. Pip was wrong; Amelia had been selected to play Mary for a reason. The sort of glamour the big girls possessed was hinted at in someone like Amelia. That was her appeal. Regardless of how nasty she was or what she did, it was impossible to refute that Amelia Forster possessed style beyond her years.

16
A Cut and a Clue

That afternoon after school, Pip and Olive walked down the street towards the hairdresser. Olive and Mog had been going to Chez Clarissa for as long as Olive could remember. Although Mog was sick and tired of the way that Clarissa cut her hair, she couldn't bear the thought of going to a hairdresser she did actually like in case Clarissa found out. *Life's tricky enough already*, Mog would say.

Olive liked going to Chez Clarissa because she loved studying the curls of wet hair swept into the corners of the salon and trying to work out which lady belonged to which hair clippings.

When they were almost there, Pip stopped outside a shop not two doors down and pressed her nose to the glass. Mannequins with engorged heads but no faces posed in a glittering conga line. Their skirts looked like squirts of fake cream.

'Let's look.'

'Pip, nothing will fit. It never does – that's why I have to shop at David Jones,' said Olive. 'In the kids' section,' she added in a whisper. 'Besides, it's a bit . . . you know.'

'What?'

'Tacky.'

Pip looked at Olive. Her eyes narrowed. 'Well, I'm going to check it out. I for one am sick of getting about in your Alice in Wonderland gear.' She stalked into the shop and picked up a slippery top lit with sequins. Then she strolled to the counter and bought it.

Olive watched on in disbelief. Pip knew they had to pay for the haircut with the money Mog had given them, but she'd still gone and bought a top *just like that*, right in front of Olive. Not only had she gone and bought a top with the hairdresser money *just like that* but she had gone and bought one that Mrs Graham would only describe as garish. Olive hated it. She glared at her sister as they left the shop, and ignored her as they walked into the salon.

'Olive Garnaut, what have you done?' Clarissa was tall and clunky, with modern jewellery and a large pile of over-dyed hair that was so dry she ran the risk of igniting whenever she turned on the hairdryer. 'Have a seat, have a seat,' she bawled across the room. A double row of women in pink plastic ponchos looked up from their magazines.

'Oh, I didn't, well actually, Pip—' Olive stuttered.

'What a lopsided job!' bellowed Clarissa, and the ladies tittered.

'Take a seat, love. I'll fix you up in no time.'

Olive smoothed her hands over her wonky hair flaps. While Clarissa was very sensitive when it came to criticism of her own hairdos, she was not as sensitive when it came to others'.

'It wasn't meant to be hurtful, Ol. Don't worry about it.' Pip sighed. She may have been trying to sound comforting, but she sounded exasperated.

'Don't worry about it? Because you went and bought a top *just like that*, I can't afford to pay,' Olive sniffed.

Pip frowned. 'We'll think of something. We'll put it on Visa. Come on, let's sit down.'

Olive walked over to the chairs in a huff. It was difficult to stay cross with Pip when Olive only had one sister and one friend, and they were actually both the same person – but she wasn't going to give in too easily.

To avoid Pip's eye, Olive picked up a magazine. Olive was extremely partial to magazines. She adored poring over the beautiful women in their strappy dresses, but she was even more riveted by the stories of people who had Conquered All to Overcome Adversity – people who had lost relatives and limbs.

Olive read studiously, trying to ignore Pip, who was frolicking in the sacred space behind the counter, examining the tester tubs of hair product on the glass shelves next to the cash register. Olive waited for Clarissa to explode, but she had found a customer who was actually willing to chat.

'Hmm, smell this.' Pip offered a dollop of goo as sweet and sticky as potted caramel to Olive, who shook her head.

Pip put a dab on her tongue. 'Yuck, that's horrible,' she said, spitting. 'How can something that smells so sugary taste so bitter?'

Olive reached for a local paper.

'I'm going to go and find some water,' Pip croaked and ran out of the room.

Olive was as fond of local papers as she was of magazines. For years she'd turfed them into the recycling pile, until Mathilda had pointed out the personal columns, lodged deep in the back of each edition. Personal columns were chat rooms for old people, Mathilda had said, and Olive had read them ever since. She ran her eyes down the column. It was full of the usual collection of what Mog called life's lonelies.

ARE YOU HER?
Was that you – blonde, cute with m'cino and WW
in Booth's Caf last Tues? Our eyes locked a-x room.
If it was, let's lock again. Rob VMB 3136.

GENTLEMAN PREFERS NO BLONDES
Mature gentleman, cultured, long-time interest in
Asia.
Wishes to meet young, slim Oriental lady to share
cultural interests. Barry VMB 7628.

ARE YOU A LONE PARENT?
Parents without Partners Tree Trimming Party
(Seaside branch) Sat 9 December 8 p.m.
Live band. No jeans. VMB 7759 for more info.

Olive tried to imagine getting Mog to attend the Parents without Partners Tree Trimming Party. No hope – Mog wouldn't go even if she could wear jeans. If Pip and Olive did start searching for their father, though, Mog's single status might be a good thing.

Olive closed her eyes and imagined a *Brady Bunch* ending to the hunt for Mustard Seed, in which he kissed Mog on the lips and swung her up and round. He then put his arms around the twins and all four of them drove to KFC, bought a family bucket of chicken, and fought over drumsticks the whole way home in the car.

Olive smiled and read on. Her eye fell on an ad under the 'Massage and Alternative Therapies' section. The ad was orange and cream and stood right out.

MUSTARD SEED NATURAL HEALTH CLINIC
SHIATSU ❋ REFLEXOLOGY ❋ HERBAL STEAM ❋
PILATES ❋ YOGA
222 HUNT STREET, WEESBOROUGH, PH. 794 6222

Mustard Seed Natural Health Clinic. Mustard Seed Natural Health Clinic. Olive felt two hands on her shoulders. 'You OK, doll? You're looking pretty pale, even by your standards.'

Olive nodded as Clarissa looped a towel and then a pink poncho around her neck.

'Now what happened here? You're the spit of Mog with that short hair.'

'A friend cut it,' Olive managed, clutching the local

paper while Clarissa rattled on about the ins and outs of home-cut hair and the dangers of using unprofessional scissors.

Olive tried to keep up with the sentences, but she couldn't. Everything around her fizzed. Mustard Seed lived there. WilliamPetersMustardSeed lived in Weesborough. He did yoga – just like Mog in the pictures.

Clarissa paused to adjust a black bib around Olive's shoulders, then sent her scissors snapping along Olive's hairline.

Olive stared at the reflection of the shop's kitchen door in the mirror, desperate for Pip. 'Clarissa, where's Weesborough, exactly?'

'Weesbowa? Lemesee. Not too far fwom 'ere. Defin'ly seaside. Thinkit's just ona nummer two twam,' replied Clarissa through a mouthful of clips.

Olive watched Pip walk back into the room and sank into a smile.

Clarissa shot off to approve another client's blow-dry. 'Gorge. Just gorgeous,' she said to the woman. 'Now let me introduce you to a new treatment we've got for those ends . . .'

Pip snorted. 'Your hair looks exactly the same. Mathilda and I could open a salon. Why did you want to know about "Weesbowa"?'

'Weesborough.' Olive pulled the paper out from under the pink plastic poncho. Pip's eyes went straight to the orange ad. 'Can my spam. It's him. It has to be. Where the bezoozus is Weesborough?'

'I already asked,' whispered Olive. 'It's not far – on the number two tramline.'

'That's this line. We passed a stop on the way here.' Pip looked as shocked as Olive felt. Olive hadn't really expected to find Mustard Seed at all – and she certainly hadn't expected to find him on their doorstep.

Olive handed the paper to her sister. The ink was smudgy where she'd held it. 'Quick, go and jot down the details.'

'Bugger that. Rip it out.' Pip lunged at the page. Olive tucked the torn piece of paper up her sleeve for safe-keeping.

'Come on, let's go.' Pip headed towards the door.

'Go? Pip, I'm still in a smock, and in case you've forgotten, I haven't paid yet.' At the very mention of payment, Olive all but forgot the excitement of the big new clue.

Pip looked up at the clock. 'Well hurry. It's him, Olive. It has to be. I'll meet you outside in five.'

Clarissa checked Olive's hair and helped her out of her poncho. 'OK, doll, that will be fifty-five dollars, please. VAT-inc.'

Olive squinted. 'Um, Clarissa, I'm . . . well, I'm really sorry, but I lost the money Mog gave me. Do you mind if I pay with the Visa card?' Olive blushed and tried to hide Pip's cardboard bag behind her knees.

Clarissa looked at the hot pink logo on the bag and winked. 'It doesn't matter, love. We share the same weakness. There's no need to use the Visa card, love – I'll just get Mog to square it up next time.'

'Thank you, Clarissa. Thanks.'

Olive tried to conceal the anger in her step as she left the salon. It *did* matter; it mattered dreadfully. Olive was responsible; she didn't share the weakness, 'love'; and she wanted to throttle her sister.

17
Square One

The twins pushed through the Friday shop-traffic. The street was full of mothers picking up last-minute chops for dinner and business people sipping beers in unravelling suits.

'OK, OK. I said I'm sorry,' said Pip. 'But how can you talk about a top at a time like this? We've found him, Olive, and we didn't even have to try. It's fate. Besides, at least I've got something to meet him in.' The bag bumped against Olive's right knee.

They walked on for a bit in silence; Olive stepping over the cracks in the pavement, Pip stepping squarely on them.

'There's the tram stop over there.' Pip pointed at the green shelter. 'Shall we go now? Just turn up and demand a Pilates?'

'It's *Pil-ar-tays*,' said Olive, pronouncing it like

someone who owned a poodle. 'Amelia's mother has it.'

'Pie-lates, Pil-ar-tays, whatever. Want to get one now?'

'Let's ring first.' Olive wanted to think. Launching right into this seemed wrong.

'Why?'

'WilliamPetersMustardSeed might not work on Fridays, and besides, it's getting late.' Although it was not the first time Olive had spoken his name out loud, it still felt foreign in her mouth – like the wads of cotton her dentist stuffed in to stop dribbling.

'Have you got your mobile on you?'

'No,' said Olive, knowing full well that it was in her bag.

Pip pointed to a phone box a little further along the street. 'I bet you haven't used one of those for a while.'

When they reached it, Olive saw that the door had been smashed and had shattered into little chunks of glass. The whole booth smelled of urine.

Pip stepped over the glass and picked up the pay phone receiver. 'Still works.' She took out the ad and crammed some coins – *Change from that tarty top*, Olive thought sourly – into the slot.

'Don't.' Olive reached up and across Pip to cut the call, but Pip blocked her. Olive stood wedged between the glass wall of the phone box and Pip's left arm.

'Mustard Seed Natural Health Clinic, this is Melé.' Even though Olive wasn't holding the phone, she heard each syllable as clearly as if the receiver had been pressed to her own ear.

'Oh, hello,' said Pip. 'I was wondering if you could help me.' She looked at Olive and pulled a hoity-toity face. She'd put on her proper voice, her charm-the-grown-ups-while-serving-*hors d'oeuvres*-at-a-cocktail-party voice; a voice that showed she knew her *vol-au-vents* from her *crudités* and always offered a *napkin* and never a *serviette*.

Pip spoke straight into the receiver. 'I'd like a pil-ar-tays for my mum. May I please come down and get one?'

'Is this a prank? Because I am getting very sick of prank calls,' the lady snapped back, uncharmed.

'No, no,' said Pip. 'She wants one, so I thought I'd get it for her birthday.'

The lady on the phone paused, then laughed. 'Oh, I'm sorry. Pilates is similar to yoga. You could buy her a course, I suppose, but pilates is not something you can giftwrap!'

'Oh, thanks. Can I – I mean, may I – come now?' Pip winked at Olive.

'Of course. Last class is at seven thirty p.m. If there isn't anyone at the desk, just ring the bell.'

The phone clicked neatly. The girls looked at each other. Stepping punctiliously over the smashed glass, they headed towards the tram stop; glass cubes flickered like crystal in their wake.

Olive and Pip found Hunt Street without too much fuss – its mouth was only two tram stops from Chez Clarissa. Hunt Street was, however, longer than Olive had expected; long and sparsely lined with skinny gum trees that cowered from the traffic-roar.

By the time the girls finally reached number 222, Pip was walking with an exaggerated limp. The cardboard bag containing the *just like that* top dragged along the ground. The girls were hot and dusty.

The Mustard Seed Natural Health Clinic was hard to miss. It was the exact middle house in a row of seven terraces linked like paper chains. It stood out because it had been painted cream and orange, while the other buildings were skimmed-milk grey. A chocolate-coloured sign soared above the fence.

Olive looked at the words MUSTARD SEED. When she was little, that name had seemed so exotic in a class where all the other dads were Lukes and Petes and Jameses. It had suggested a father who travelled; who read; who could reel off the names of one hundred and one spices. But now, here in the suburbs, it just seemed silly.

'Well, this is it.' Olive smoothed her skirt. She wished that they'd thought this through; it was all too rushed. A girl should never go to meet her father for the first time with freshly cut hair stuck to the back of her neck.

Pip marched confidently up the front stairs, apparently oblivious to dust and hair clippings. Olive followed.

Twelve Tibetan bells chimed as the girls walked into the Mustard Seed Natural Health Clinic. Inside, it was at once wholesome and luxurious. The furniture was low and wooden and covered in plump canvas cushions.

A woman with loose white trousers and skin the

colour of almonds wafted into the reception to greet them. She put her hands in a praying position and lowered her forehead to her fingertips.

'*Namaste*,' she said with a voice that was deep and nutty. Her limbs were long and floppy under the white linen; her skin, eyes and hair all shone. She smiled to reveal big square teeth. Olive could tell immediately that she was the sort of woman who enjoyed her bran. 'How can I help with your journey?'

'I'd like to make an appointment for my mother – for pie-lates,' said Pip, reverting back to her charming voice, but saying it wrong again.

'Pil-ar-tays,' corrected Olive.

'I rang before.'

'Oh, yes,' said the woman. 'Melé mentioned it.' She smiled again; her smile was smooth and deep and slow.

'That's pil-ar-tays with Mustard Seed,' said Pip.

The woman tucked a piece of hair behind her ear; silver rings slid about her slender fingers. Olive could smell hand cream scented with cloves and citrus.

'Why Mustard Seed?' She wobbled her head from side to side.

'No reason.' Pip smiled a smile to match her *vol-au-vent* voice.

'I guess everybody knows that he's good,' said Olive, completely mesmerized.

'She.' The woman laughed. Her voice rang about the creamy ceilings. 'I am Mustard Seed.'

✳ ✳ ✳

'I can't believe it. I just can't believe it,' Pip bellowed down the street. 'How many freaks changed their name to Mustard Seed?'

'Mog once represented a go-go dancer called Mango-Tango.' Olive held her arms out and whipped her hips around in a hoola-hoop loop.

'"Mango-Tango" sounds zesty. Mustard Seed isn't even a nice name. I just cannot believe it.'

Olive couldn't believe that they'd just put one hundred and eighty dollars worth of pilates lessons on the Visa Card for Emergencies. Mog would hit the roof.

'I *am Mustard Seed. I* am *Mustard Seed. That is so very kind of you,*' mimicked Pip, her head knocking from side to side. '*Tell me about your journey.*' The girls stopped walking and held their tummies. They laughed until they cramped.

'Oh well.' Olive looked at her scruffy sister. Pip's hem was flapping at the bottom of her uniform and her hair-band had slipped so far down her ponytail that there was more hair in her eyes than under the elastic. 'We were completely unprepared. Mustard Seed would never have wanted us in this state.' The battered bag with the *just like that* top swung between them.

'Okey Doke's?' the twins asked each other at exactly the same time. Throwing their heads back and laughing again, they headed down to the beach.

18
Back to Square One

On Monday at lunch time, Olive walked into the library. Pip was stuck fast to the Internet. Mog had worked all weekend after all, so they hadn't been able to get near her computer.

After the unveiling of Ms Mustard Seed, Olive had been ready to call it quits. Pip, however, had the perseverance of a marathon runner. She had stared at their faces in the bathroom mirror, claiming she was trying to construct an identikit portrait of Mustard Seed from those features that she *knew for sure* weren't Mog's.

'This forehead is definitely not Garnaut,' Pip had said. 'It makes our eyes look like fish in a fishbowl.'

Olive had rolled her eyes. 'Mog's got the forehead, too – it's just hidden under her fringe.'

Even if the forehead was Mog's, it was weird to think

that there was somebody out there, an unknown, who shared other traits with them.

Olive pulled up a chair beside Pip. 'I knew you were desperate to research, but I didn't think you'd miss most of the day.'

'Oh, hi, Ol.' Pip leaned back on her chair. 'I only missed the morning. Anyway, one of the subjects was PE, which doesn't really count.'

Olive tucked her hair behind her ears. 'Did you find anything?'

'I'm just about to do some research into the Department of Marine Assets and Biology for the lighthouse. Look . . .'

Olive peered over Pip's shoulder.

'Where's the clue folder?' Pip asked.

'In the bag.' Olive pulled it out and stared at the bundle of papers between them on the table.

'It says here that there are twenty-three lighthouses in Victoria,' said Pip. 'Fifteen are still in use today. None were built after 1902.'

'So that means we have to look at eight abandoned lighthouses,' Olive cut in. 'We'll never find him.' She pulled her knees up to her chest, then pulled her jumper over them and rocked.

'No, it's a bit easier. Of those, three are still used for "tourism", which leaves six.'

'Five,' corrected Olive. 'You should pay attention in Maths.' Pip had taken to Maths like an Eskimo to a boogie board. She was no natural. Olive put her chin on the top of a knee that was protruding through the

V-neck of her jumper. 'So what are the lighthouses called?'

Pip rolled her eyes. 'Can I finish?'

Olive leaned forward to peek at the screen.

'Of the *five* remaining' – Pip paused for emphasis – 'three are described as being bluestone.'

'And we know, from the photo, that Mustard Seed's lighthouse has a limestone base.' Olive smiled.

'Which leaves two: Port Stirling, and Port Wilson,' Pip concluded.

Two lighthouses. Olive felt weary just thinking about it. Two was better than eight, but Olive still had blisters from the journey to the fake Mustard Seed at 222 Hunt Street. She put her feet back down on the floor, and the grey woollen bosoms that her knees had formed disappeared. 'So which one is it?'

'I'm not sure,' said Pip. 'Neither of them are on the Internet – no pictures whatsoever.'

Olive clicked into the catalogue website.

'Look, there's a book on Australian lighthouses in the R-section of the library.' Pip pointed at the screen. 'Come and help me pinch it.'

'Are you kidding?'

The R-section of the library was the reserve section. The Rs meant that the books could only be read in the library under the strict supervision of Mrs Steif.

Mrs Steif had liver-coloured hair, thick block-toed shoes and the reflexes of a panther. Shoulders square, nose twitching, she joggled in front of the reserve section, guarding the shelves and their contents like a soccer goalie. Mrs Steif was often heard boasting (in a thick German accent) that under her watch, library theft had been reduced by thirty-seven per cent per annum.

'Come on, Olive. It will only take five minutes and I've got a plan.'

Olive looked over her shoulder to make sure that none of Mrs Steif's assistants were eavesdropping. They could be hard to spot, those assistants. While girls such as Nut Allergy were obvious library recruits, it was rumoured that Mrs Steif, drawing on her experiences in the former Eastern Bloc, had library moles operating *undercover*.

Mrs Steif and her hench-girls engendered no fear in Pip whatsoever. 'Come on. I'll start eating a banana or chewing gum or something, and she'll get so worked up about it, you can stuff the book under your jumper and run through the door – home free.'

Olive moved over to the R-section and pulled the lighthouse book down from the shelves. She opened the index. 'Port Stirling – page thirty-two!' Olive turned to the right page. There wasn't a picture of Port Stirling lighthouse, but there was a small description that echoed the website. 'And look – here's Port Wilson, too!'

'See if there's a map.' Pip's voice tinkled like lemonade.

At the front of the book there was a map of Victoria. It had been cut from the rest of Australia and floated on the page like a hunk of cake. A number of lighthouses were marked on it.

The bell rang.

'Crap.' Pip looked up. 'What have you got on now?'

'Maths with Mr Hollywood. You going to come?'
Olive didn't like to suggest that Pip's earlier struggle with
basic arithmetic implied that she ought to.

Pip paused. As one of the only two male teachers in
the school, Mr Hollywood was the subject of numerous
crushes, despite the blond tips in his hair. It was
rumoured that Mrs Steif adored him. Pip did, too.

'OK, I'll come, but I'm not sitting anywhere *near*
Amelia.' Pip handed the lighthouse book to her sister.
'Are you ready to make a run for it?'

'No way, Pip. I'll copy the map. We can even do it in
colour.'

Pip rolled her eyes. 'You're way too honest – you'd
make a lousy jewel thief.'

Olive watched her sister from the photocopier and
smiled. Pip was leapfrogging the metal poles that held up
the velvet queue-rope in front of the borrowing desk. It
was strange, thought Olive, but even though Pip loathed
them, with all her bravado and crazy ideas, Pip was
exactly the sort of girl Amelia and Mathilda would
like.

When the girls walked into the classroom, Mr
Hollywood was swaggering about rearranging desks.
Unlike Ms Stable-East, he preferred a horseshoe con-
figuration. *Opens up the channels. Much more conducive to
natter*, he said. There was a band of dust across his
bottom where he had leaned up against the whiteboard.

Mr Hollywood didn't address the girls as they walked
in. Pip moaned. 'This is hopeless.'

'Pip! He's gross,' said Olive. 'He's ancient and he's married.' Olive took out her maths book.

Pip pulled out the clue folder. 'He looks straight through me.'

'If you studied long division as hard as you study that, he might notice you.'

'I just want the right lighthouse. It's going to be hard enough to get there without picking the dud.' Pip placed the map on her desk.

The afternoon buzz rose. Mr Hollywood tapped his ruler on the board. 'OK, girls, Lunch is Over Now, so That Will Do. Let's turn to Page Forty-Six.' Like all teachers at the Joanne d'Arc School for Girls, Mr Hollywood had a propensity to talk in capitals.

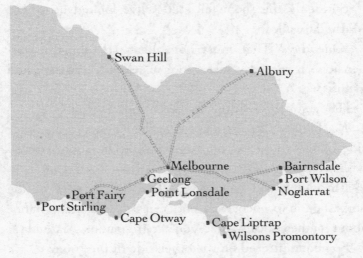

Olive moved the map onto her Maths homework and angled her head so that Amelia was in her blind spot. She surveyed the wheat-coloured land. Port Stirling was nowhere near Port Wilson. Olive traced her finger in a line from one to the other. She'd learned from trips to junk shops with Mog that maps were tricky. On a map, a crescent of road the size of her fingernail could translate to hours along the asphalt.

'Look.' Olive pointed. 'Port Fairy – just like Mog's T-shirt. It's not too far from Stirling.'

Pip pulled the map so close to her face that Olive was sure her breath would make it soggy. 'You're right, Ol. So the Port Fairy Folk Festival was not actually a fairy gathering at all.' Pip's cheeks were rosy. 'Do you reckon that's the one?'

'That *must* be it. It makes sense.' Olive carefully added the clue to their list: *Port Stirling*.

Suddenly the room fell still. Olive looked up to see Mathilda walk in.

'One day? That must have been the shortest suspension on record – just a long weekend,' Pip said and grunted.

'They got those Saturday detentions as well.'

Mathilda walked straight past their desks to the other side of the room, where Amelia sat. The room rustled with whispers.

Mr Hollywood coughed. 'While the purpose of the horseshoe is to encourage natter, it's to encourage natter about mathematics. Would you care to join us, Mathilda?'

Someone tittered on the other side of the room.

Pip sighed. 'He looks so handsome when he's angry.'

Olive rolled her eyes and ignored her sister for the rest of the lesson. *Stirling. Stirling. He lives in a lighthouse at Port*

Stirling. She let the name tingle on the tip of her tongue. It felt silvery and romantic, but somehow regal at the same time.

At the end of the lesson, Pip was in such a deep swoon that she barely stirred. It was a bit off, thought Olive, a crush like that. She prodded her sister and looked at her watch. 'We've got Science.'

Pip groaned. 'I'm not coming.'

Mrs Dixon did not tip her hair and lacked all Mr Hollywood's charisma.

'It's not that bad,' said Olive, but her voice was drowned by the screech of chair legs on linoleum. Year 7C was moving to Science, and Pip was already out of the door.

Olive zipped her pencil case closed and pulled the loose pages of the clue folder into some sort of order.

'Olive,' called Mr Hollywood from the front of the room. 'You've got neat writing. Could you lend Mathilda and Amelia your long-division notes from Friday, please?'

Olive looked up. Amelia was leaning over her desk. Her arms were thin but strong from sun and sport.

'Yes, Mr Hollywood,' said Olive. *Why me, Mr Hollywood?* thought Olive.

Amelia loomed right over the open clue folder and tipped her head. 'What's that?' She was smiling sweetly – suspiciously sweetly, as Ms Stable-East always said.

'Um, what?' Olive placed her pencil case over the folder, but it was too narrow.

'That.' Amelia started to read through a coin-slot

smile. 'Clues, WilliamPetersMustardSeed . . . what? Adverse possession, tie-dye, Port Fairy. A map? What's *that* all about?'

'Nothing.'

'Sure.' Amelia's dimples shimmered.

Mathilda came up behind Amelia and put her chin on Amelia's shoulder. 'Did you get them?'

Mr Hollywood walked over. 'Not the extension exercises, Olive, just Friday's notes.' He turned to Amelia. 'Next time you're asked to see Mrs Dalling, Amelia, I suggest you try to do so in your own time.'

'Here you go.' Olive handed Amelia her notes.

Amelia managed a half-nod, then she and Mathilda locked arms and laughs and walked out into the afternoon.

Olive looked back down at her clues. *Stirling, Stirling.* She rolled the word, his word, around her mouth. It was still effervescent. Nothing could collapse it.

19
The Port Fairy Find

Later that afternoon, the kitchen was hazy with smoke. Pip had decided that they should cook, and cartons of milk and split bags of sugar were crammed onto the already crammed bench. Batter dripped onto the kitchen floor, and the marble slab was peppered with black crumbs.

Olive looked around. 'Mog's going to kill us.' She picked a wooden spoon and three eggshells off one of Mog's binders. 'I told you she's fussy about her work.'

'Whoops,' said Pip and laughed.

Olive tripped over some stray pots and pans that had tumbled onto the floor with a crash earlier.

'Hey, I found that in the fridge.' Pip gestured at one of Mog's mobiles with her elbow. 'In the butter compartment.'

Olive picked up the cold phone. There were forty-two

missed calls. At least it was still working – Mog had thrown her last mobile in with a white wash.

Pip offered Olive a beater. The best cake-mix streaks had already been licked. 'Do you think I could have the phone if Mog doesn't want it?'

'You can keep it. Mog has a couple of spares. We'll just need to get a new SIM card.' Mog had a collection of mobiles like other mothers had collections of luggage sets, charms or French provincial pudding basins. Olive wiped batter from the phone screen and passed it over the bench.

'Ta-da.' Pip pointed at a tray piled with dark, crooked cakes, speckled with hundreds and thousands. 'Fairy cakes in honour of the Port Fairy Find.'

Olive rubbed her eyes. Hundreds and thousands were caught in her eyelashes. 'What are hundreds and thousands?' She sank her teeth into a cake so tough that burnt bits scratched the roof of her mouth.

'Smartie poo,' said Pip. 'Bad joke. Very J-school.'

Olive picked up a cloth and started to clean. Unfortunately, Pip had left it so dirty that Olive was only rearranging the gunk into ridged smears.

'Can you pass the map?' Pip asked. 'I want to check out Port Stirling again.'

Olive flipped through the clue folder with one hand while she scrubbed at a spot of hardened batter with the other.

'That's strange. It's not here. It must have got mixed up with my stuff in Maths or Science or something. I'll check my locker tomorrow.'

'But I want to look at it now, Ol – see how to get there.'

Olive sighed. Pip could be very wearisome. 'I'll have a look in the study to see if there's another map, if you put the rubbish out.'

'I *hate* garbage,' said Pip as if she had been asked to deal with nothing else since her arrival, and she pranced out of the back door. Olive took the opportunity to dispose of the rest of her cake, which dropped to the bottom of the bin with a most unfairylike thud. She rinsed the cloth and stared at her runny reflection in the corrugated sink.

It was funny. As soon as Pip left, the house was silent, but silence no longer ached or muzzled; it just settled on and around Olive, as fine and gentle as pollen.

Mog's library was stacked with books. Some stood straight and tall on the shelves in two-by-two rows; others had been crammed in above them, so tightly that their covers buckled. Mog said the library was a bit like her life: it had started out neat and ended up all over the place.

Olive read through the books' leather spines: *Commonwealth Law Reports*, *Victorian Law Reports*, *Australian Criminal Reports*. Right at the far end of the bottom shelf, near a pile of magazines, was another book with a hard cover: *Victorian Maps: Tripping through the Garden State by Rail and Road*.

Bingo-bango.

The book was split by a thin ribbon. Olive opened it

at the marked page. There on the map, circled in biro, was not Port Stirling but Port Wilson lighthouse. Next to it was also a note in Mog's scribble: *Sandy track, approx. 1 hr, take water*.

'Pip. Hey, Piiip, check this out!' Olive bellowed. Pip bounded into the study. She looked at Mog's scribble, then flicked to Port Stirling in the index. The brittle pages of Map 47 creaked, and the smell of ink welled. It had never been opened.

'What do you think?' asked Olive. 'Wilson or Stirling?'

'I think we were wrong,' said Pip. I think it's Wilson – which means she must have travelled mighty far to kiss that fairy at Port Fairy.'

'Or she borrowed the T-shirt.' Olive was surprised it hadn't occurred to her before. Mog said all her clothes were second-hand in those days, which was why, despite all their knick-knacks, Mog was keen on new clothing now.

'I'm just glad we didn't hitch all the way over there.'

Olive nodded, although she had never had any intention of hitchhiking. She ran her finger along the road to Port Wilson lighthouse. In her dreamings, the lighthouse was whitewashed and airy. She'd imagined a soaring roof with wooden beams, like the inside of a cathedral; a galley kitchen with bags of spices pegged shut and bulk tubs of margarine, like the kitchen at school camp. She'd imagined chairs with seats smooth from wear, and hammocks to rock in. She hadn't imagined it would be so far away. 'It's still a long way.'

Pip looked as depressed as one of the cupcakes. 'I think Noglarrat's the nearest big town.' She pointed to a spot where the roads converged into an artery.

'Well, I guess we've got to get to Noglarrat,' said Olive as if there could be nothing simpler for two girls not that far into their double digits.

Pip brightened immediately. 'Without Mog noticing,' she said, just as confidently.

'Or Ms Stable-East.'

'We could collect that van from the car park – I'd get better at it if we practised.'

Olive remembered the dirty bunion flip-flop under the pedals. 'It's not ours, Pip. Anyway, I might die down there, or catch tinea or some other disgusting fungal disease.'

Pip's nostrils flared. 'You have to get over these hygiene issues.'

'Over? You don't get *over* hygiene issues. You might get over a cold, but hygiene is important.' Olive could feel the vein in her forehead throb.

'You'll never be able to have a boyfriend, Olive. You simply can't have your hygiene standards and any sort of interest in boys – they stink like salami sandwiches left in a school bag for six weeks. With any luck, you'll be a lesbian.'

The study was quiet. Pip tapped the map with a finger as fine and pale as one of Mog's cigarettes. 'Should we hitch?'

Olive shook her head. Hopping into a car with people they didn't know spelled Stranger Danger. Olive wasn't that dumb.

153

A black line much like a stitched scar cut across the page.

'That must be a train track,' said Pip. 'We could catch a train to Noglarrat and then figure it out.'

'OK.' Olive was not convinced, although arguably they *could* run away from Stranger Danger in a train – or at least leap onto the roof or fly out of the window into a butter-yellow paddock. 'But we'll have to find some money. I don't want Mog to read it on her statement. She'd freak.'

'Mog reads bank statements?'

Olive shrugged. It was true that it was difficult to imagine. Mog did not seem, and was in fact not, the finicky bank-statement-double-checking type. She took more of an it-will-all-come-out-in-the-wash approach to finance, unlike Mrs Graham, who checked off every item on her receipts with a tick and went back to the super-market when she was short-corn-canned.

'She reads them sometimes, but not as often as she says she should. She thinks banks are shifty. She's worked against a couple of them.' Olive picked up the map book and headed for the kitchen. 'She doesn't trust banks, weathermen, or anybody who works in real estate and calls themself a professional.'

Pip nodded. Even she had nothing to add.

20
Changing Places

The next day at school, Olive ducked out of Pastoral Care to find her diary. Pastoral Care was taught by Macca, who looked more like a teenage babysitter than a minister, which she in fact was. Macca was an anomaly at the Joanne d'Arc School for Girls, and from the first lesson, Olive had been transfixed. She had expected a minister to speak of nothing but God and wear a white-collared robe and probably even metal underpants. Macca, however, had blue hair extensions, played the banjo, and talked about social justice. While Olive had learned little about Buddhism or the meaning of cows to Hindus (Macca preferred songs to the syllabus), she had learned that ministers didn't always look like ministers.

Olive wandered through the cloakroom, humming 'Kumbaya'. The lockers were in two rows: top and bottom.

Top lockers were prized, because the girls didn't have to stoop to open them, but Olive's was on the bottom. It didn't really bother her. Top or bottom, they still had the distinctive middle school smell of rust, dirty gym gear and decaying homework.

Olive rifled through the shelves of her locker, looking for her diary. It had a hard dark green cover with the school's emblem monogrammed in gold across the front and a special sticker for body spray that Mathilda had found in some magazine. It also contained her homework for Pastoral Care.

Olive was searching slowly. There was something very peaceful about school grounds with no students – something peaceful and not at all lonely. Somehow the knowledge that other girls were nearby made it a genuine place of rest.

Just as Olive was pondering this, Mathilda walked past. She looked at Olive. Her eyes ducked to the side and then to the floor. 'Oh. Hi,' she mumbled.

Olive peered around; Amelia was nowhere in sight.

'Are you wagging?' Mathilda looked incredulous.

'No,' said Olive. 'No, I'm not. I'm . . . I'm just trying to find something.'

'Oh.'

'My diary. You know, the one with that scratch-and-sniff sticker you stuck on it. The body-spray one that smells like pudding.'

Mathilda shrugged and looked awkward and then irritated, in a way that made it clear it was far too early to be discussing shared pasts, especially in public. She then walked off towards the classrooms with her pigeon-toed walk.

'Oh well. Great to speak to you.' Olive stared at Mathilda's back until it disappeared round the corner.

'And that's all she said?'

Olive had convened a crisis meeting at lunch to discuss the exchange with her sister, who had failed to show up for Pastoral Care.

'Yep. She said "Oh," "Are you wagging?" and then "Oh" (again), but it was fine. There were lots of meaningful gaps in between.'

'Meaningful gaps? Olive, are you mad? She was monosyllabic – rude to you,' Pip spluttered. 'Did she at least say whether *she* was wagging?'

'Nope.'

'Did you ask?'

'Nope. There wasn't time. It was over so quickly.'

'Olive, you're useless sometimes. We could have got her in trouble, got her back.'

Olive swallowed and tried not to look shocked. 'Pip. That's not in the spirit of things. She's my best friend.'

Pip rolled her eyes and moved away from Olive. 'Charming.'

'Oh, come off it, Pip. Not like that. She *was* my best friend, I mean.' Olive reached out for her sister's arm. Pip pulled away.

'Remember your plait?'

Olive rolled the greaseproof paper down her sausage roll. 'It's just that I don't want more trouble. Besides, maybe Mathilda's changed? Maybe she was just there enjoying the peace of the empty locker room, too? Maybe she'd also lost something? I didn't ask.'

Olive liked the thought that both she and Mathilda, despite the dumping, might be leading lives in parallel lines; lines that could perhaps move together one day. True parallel lines never met – like tram tracks. But Olive knew that sets of parallel lines could cross – sometimes even over and over, like the paths of slalom skiers – and maybe Olive and Pip, as a pair, would one day cross Mathilda and Amelia's tracks again.

Pip shook her head. 'Like you as I do, sometimes I worry whether all your oars are in the water.'

Olive sniffed and looked away.

'Look at that.' Pip pointed at two girls sitting on a bench to their left. Nut Allergy and her sister, the Nut Allergy Facsimile, were eating cheese-slice sandwiches. Nut Allergy's sister was in junior school. She had exactly the same matted hair and orthotic lace-up shoes, just in a smaller size. Unlike Nut Allergy, she was meant to be smart. Her real name was Melanie, but she was called the Nut Allergy Facsimile or Smelly Melly.

Nut Allergy and Smelly Melly weren't speaking, but they didn't look unhappy.

'Isn't that social death, to sit with your sister at lunch time?' asked Pip through a mouthful of pastry. Neither Pip nor Olive commented on the inescapable fact that there was nobody without the surname Garnaut in their own elite circle à deux.

'I guess if you're Nut Allergy, it's a question of where

else there is to go.' Olive took another bite of her sausage roll. Sauce shot out of the bottom of the soggy bag and onto the bricks, where it lay like evidence in a crime scene.

'I wonder if they play Dungeons and Dragons?' asked Pip.

Suddenly, something in Olive twitched. It was an epiphany — a series of little facts and conversations which converged in her mind to form something solid. 'Pip, I've just remembered something.'

'What?' Pip was trying to rub tomato sauce off the T of Olive's T-bar, but had only succeeded in transferring it onto Olive's socks through the petal-shaped cut-outs.

'Nut Allergy. Her name is Kate.'

Olive knew that she should feel outraged, incensed, even violated: Nut Allergy was a social climber of the most grotesque and conniving kind. Fancy telling her father that she, lowly Nut Allergy, ate lunch with her, Olive Garnaut, formerly of the greater Year 7 middle class.

Instead, however, Olive just felt sad.

21
The Salami Vegetarian

That afternoon, the twins dumped their school bags at home and headed straight to Woolworths to shop for provisions for their trip. This was the only domestic task Olive had seen Pip apply herself to with any sort of dedication. Although they still hadn't agreed on a date, Pip was adamant that they be prepared. It was funny: the longer they had to think about it, the more they needed to organize – when they'd taken nothing at all to see the fake Mustard Seed.

At the shop, the girls bought bottled water, a torch, batteries and chocolate for energy. Olive remembered something called 'scroggin' she'd read about in a camping book. It was a mix of chocolate, dried fruit, nuts and seeds, but as neither of them particularly liked dried fruit, nuts or seeds, they ditched those bits.

Pip spotted some freeze-dried beef stroganoffs. They

opened one of the boxes to have a peek. It really was amazing to think that an entire beef stroganoff could be squeezed into such a small bag. The beef stroganoff was brown with orange bits in it – like vomit.

'It's sucking in its cheeks in disgust.' Olive poked the plastic. The stroganoff was as rigid as a ski boot.

'We'd have to be in a real emergency to eat that.' Pip nudged the bag. 'Especially since I'm vegetarian.'

Olive turned to her sister. 'You are not vegetarian.' Olive knew about vegetarians. Mog was vegetarian and before that she had been vegan, which was a stricter kind of vegetarian who didn't eat honey or wear leather shoes. Not that it had mattered to Mog though, as in those days she hadn't worn shoes anyway. Pip, on the other hand, did wear shoes, and for a pretty skinny kid she was a complete guts who devoured everything she was served (and half of Olive's) – including the meaty parts.

'I am, too,' protested Pip.

'Since when?'

'Since always.'

'But you eat salami.' Olive recalled the hoses of salami that hung on hooks in the local deli. At the weekend, Pip had chowed through most of a salami before they'd even made it home.

'Salami doesn't count. I am vegetarian for everything other than tasty sausages.'

'And chicken.'

'Oh. Some chicken,' said Pip thoughtfully.

'And fish,' Olive pushed.

'OK. And fish, but only with batter.'

'I think you just don't eat steak.'

'Or freeze-dried beef that looks like vomit.'

Olive took the frozen stroganoff back from her sister. 'Even if we were facing death by starvation?'

Pip looked Olive up and then down. She grabbed three beef stroganoffs (one for Mustard Seed) and tossed them back in the trolley. 'Good point. I reckon I'd eat them over you, anyway. More meat.'

The girls walked along the aisles, heads tilted to the side, browsing for anything they might have forgotten. All the products looked crisp and shiny under the white, white supermarket light.

'The problem with planning,' said Pip, 'is that you only ever plan to do what you feel like doing at the time you actually make the plan. At the moment I feel like chocolate, but how do I know what I'll want to eat when we're on the road? I might want chips. It's so much easier to play things by ear. You mind the trolley. I'm just going to check out the lolly aisle again.' Pip headed off towards aisle three.

'Hello there.'

Olive looked straight up and into the pink-frosted lips of Mrs Graham. She sidled around to the front of the trolley so that Mrs Graham wouldn't see the freeze-dried beef stroganoffs and get suspicious or, even worse, think that they were the type of girls to eat freeze-dried beef stroganoffs when there wasn't an emergency. 'Hello, Mrs Graham.'

Mrs Graham had a bulk packet of toilet paper sticking out of the top of her trolley. It made Olive feel embarrassed. Knowing that her friend's mother bought toilet paper twenty-four rolls at a time seemed indecently intimate.

Mrs Graham leaned over Olive and peered into their trolley. 'Are you going camping?'

Olive nodded and smiled.

'With Mog?' The pink-frosted lips dropped open. 'I thought Mog hated camping.'

'No, no. With my father, actually.'

'Oh.' Mrs Graham looked rattled, as if there were a number of things she expected of the Garnauts at the weekend, and none of them involved anything as functional as a family camping trip with a father who was supposed to be unknown and/or absent.

'Well,' said Mrs Graham. 'Won't that be fun.' She tipped her head to the side and blinked.

Olive blinked back.

'Well, I hope we'll see you soon then,' said Mrs Graham and steered her cart down PASTA/SPREADS/KITCHEN UTENSILS. Olive watched her floppy navy bottom lumber, then pause. Mrs Graham reached for a family pack of shell pasta and turned. 'Olive, what was the name of your father again?'

'William,' said Olive. 'William Peters.'

'William,' said Mrs Graham, chewing on the name, looking as if she'd expected something a little more unusual, a little more flamboyant, a little more like *Mustard Seed*. 'Well, have fun, dear,' she said and wheeled out of sight.

Pip jogged back towards Olive. 'Who was that?'

'Mrs Graham.'

Pip frowned. 'What did she want?'

'Nothing, I just bumped into her. It was completely uncomfy – like talking to somebody with poppy seeds in their teeth. I wasn't quite sure where to look.'

'She buys gherkins,' said Pip. 'That fact alone has confirmed all of my prejudices about that family.'

'Do you think we should take Mustard Seed a present?' Olive was keen to stay clear of the subject of Mrs Graham. She couldn't believe she'd gone and blabbed about Mustard Seed, but she'd wanted Mrs Graham to admire *them* for once. She could only hope that Mrs Graham would never tell Mathilda and never ever tell Mog.

'A present? Are you kidding? By my calculations, he owes us each twelve birthdays and eleven Christmases.'

'I just don't think we should turn up empty-handed.' Olive lunged at the trolley to stop it from ploughing through a pyramid of lime marmalade.

Pip batted Olive's hands off the red handles. 'Well, I guess. If you want.'

'Mog doesn't like it when I buy her presents. She thinks it's much more thoughtful to make them.'

'I saw all those pinch pots in the kitchen,' said Pip. 'I figured no shop would sell those.' Mog had kept every clay pot Olive had ever made. Most sat coiled on the mantelpiece in the kitchen like brown snakes (according to Mog) or dog poo (according to Olive).

'What about an ashtray? We could make him one. If he's anything like Mog, he'll use it,' said Pip.

'Nah,' said Olive. 'It's an OK idea, but it's not brilliant. This has to be really special. It has to have something of us in it.' Olive scanned the supermarket shelves – brown rice, arborio rice, polenta, couscous. It wasn't much to go on. 'What about job coupons? Our class made them for Father's Day, and apparently they were a real hit. Each coupon had a promise on it: to make breakfast in bed, clean the car or polish shoes.' Olive paused. 'I gave mine to Mog.'

Pip bit her thumbnail. 'I hate Father's Day, too.'

They pushed the trolley together in silence. Girls with fathers could never understand how bare Father's Day could be. Olive imagined it was like being Jewish or Muslim on Christmas Day, when Santa Claus only brought presents for the Christian kids – even the kids who had never set foot in a church.

Olive pulled up her socks. 'Not for long. If we can make it to Port Wilson, next year will be different. Next year we'll both be able to make presents in Art that say "I ♡ Dad".'

That night at home, the twins sat around the kitchen table making a cardboard frame. They had decided to give WilliamPetersMustardSeed photographs they'd taken in an automatic photo booth in the shopping centre. They'd stuck out their tongues and pushed their cheeks together and the booth had spat out a strip of sticky photos. Then they had both stuck a fingerprint on the bottom of the strip before it dried.

'For authenticity,' Olive had said. 'Sort of an autograph – like real artists.'

Olive had started the cardboard frame four times, but she was using a pair of kitchen scissors with a slight lean, and no matter how hard she tried, the edges curved.

'It doesn't matter,' said Pip. 'Nobody but you can notice. Think of it as an arc rather than a lean.'

But it did matter, *because* Olive noticed. The tilted edges gave the frame a homemade feel, and Olive wanted it to look professional. She picked the best of the four and drew olive trees and olives with pips and hearts around the outside.

'That was a brilliant idea, the pip and olive bit,' said Pip as Olive wrapped the framed photos in tissue paper. 'Really clever. He's going to love it.'

While Olive tidied up the craft box, Pip sat watching television. Coloured light jumped about the wall as it did when they had a Christmas tree. Mog didn't like fake Christmas trees, because they didn't smell, and she didn't like cut ones, because it was cruel to butcher a tree for a few days' use. Instead, they had a tree in a pot in the garden.

'Want to help me move the Christmas tree inside tomorrow?' Olive asked Pip. 'It's a bit of a monster, but the two of us might be able to manage.' In the quick dark before a flare of advertisements, Olive saw them all collected around the base of a perfectly straight tree, hanging baked biscuits and candles on the branches like the Grahams did. The image was so clear, Olive could smell pine and nutmeg.

'Nah, I thought we should go to the lighthouse the day

after tomorrow, so we'll need tomorrow night to get organized.'

Olive's pine and nutmeg dream crumbled. 'But that's Thursday. What about the concert?' While shopping for provisions for their trip and making the frame had been fun, somehow the whole expedition had felt like a far-flung whim. In naming a day, Pip had made it solid.

'Mog's not going to the concert, remember. We can turn up late to dinner and blame it on the show.'

Olive pressed the remote control to turn down the volume. 'What about school? We've got rehearsals. They'll notice if we're not there.'

Pip's eyes didn't move from the television. 'We'll ring the school in the morning and tell them we caught a bug, so Ms Stable-East doesn't call Mog. We can figure the note bit out later. If you tell Mog that night that we needed a duvet day, she'll probably feel so guilty she wasn't around, she'll write one.'

'Pip, you're terrible,' said Olive, but she knew Pip was also right. Once Olive had felt sick and had come home from school in a taxi at lunch time. That night, Mog had blushed, kissed her and brought her a thick, fizzy vitamin drink in bed. She'd said that if Olive ever felt sick again, she could come into Chambers and lie on the couch with a hottie, regardless of what Mog had on.

'Besides, if we ring Mog *before* she heads off to the Attorney-General dinner, we won't have to go to that at all,' said Pip.

'Good-o,' said Olive. 'We'll try for Thursday. As soon

as Mog goes to work, we'll catch the tram into the city and take it from there. I guess.'

Olive tried to make her voice sound as tough as the hot-chip boys who sat on Mrs Stewart's fence. She wanted her sister to think that she was cool with it – that she was cool with a three-hour train trip to the country when they should be at school – but her voice wavered.

'We can call school from the city,' said Pip. 'It will still be so early, we can just leave a message.'

Olive noticed that Pip's voice didn't waver at all.

22
May Day

The next day, Olive and Pip were late to school. Again.

'Why are you so slow in the mornings?' Olive asked. 'You know I hate being late. It's selfish.'

'You should just go without me,' Pip struck back. 'Besides, you're just cranky because it's Wednesday.'

Mog called Wednesday the mid-week hump. *People are ratty until they get over the mid-week hump*, she always said.

The school grounds were empty but for a chip packet and a forgotten shin pad. Olive felt panicky. She breathed in little puffs.

Year 7C was in the gym, practising for the Christmas concert. Olive dropped her bag and blazer discreetly at the entrance. She needn't have bothered; the hall was in pandemonium. The microphone was howling, as were a bunch of Grade 3 choir shepherds who had lost their sheep. Ms Stable-East was sitting uncomfortably on the stage with her varicose-veined ankles dangling all bumpy over the edge. She was talking too close to the micro-phone, trying to appear both relaxed *and* in control for the benefit of Mrs Dalling, the headmistress (who did not look convinced).

'Why have they got them here?' Pip pointed to the J-school kids.

'Remember it's the *Centennial* Christmas Concert, so they want everyone involved. And they can reach the high notes.'

Ms Stable-East bellowed at the Grade 3 choir shepherds, somewhat unhelpfully, to 'ship up or shape out', and the microphone screeched again. Pip stuck her fingers in her ears. 'I can't stand the feedback,' she yelled, twice as loudly as the microphone.

Just near Pip and Olive stood Mrs Steif. She was ear-bashing Mr Hollywood about the strengths of the Dewey Decimal System. Mr Hollywood looked riveted.

'Are they flirting?'

Olive shrugged.

'I'll wait outside.' Pip slung her bag over her shoulder and turned away, looking disgusted.

'Don't leave me.' Olive grabbed at the back of Pip's jumper. 'Please.'

Pip shook her head. 'I don't want to watch. Not that.' She motioned to Mr Hollywood and Mrs Steif. 'You'll be fine, Ol.'

'Good-o.' Olive let out a shaky sigh.

Pip raised one eyebrow. 'I'll rephrase that. You'll be fine as long as you drop the "Good-o". It's really mumsy.'

'Oh.'

'Seriously, Ol, just come and get me if you need to.'

Olive watched Pip leave. The door swung behind her. She wondered if – hoped that – Pip had forgotten something, that she would return. She hadn't – didn't.

Olive stood by herself, waiting for instructions. Around her, girls huddled in bunches of threes and fours, their year groups all mixed up, tossed like salad.

'Olive. Hey, Olive, come over here,' someone shouted. Olive looked up and squinted. It was Mathilda. She and Amelia were surveying the room, perched up on the uneven bars at the back of the hall like queens on a throne.

'Me?' asked Olive, as if she were surrounded by a great horde of other Olives. Mathilda nodded and waved her over.

Olive walked towards them. Perhaps Mathilda had decided to let her back in, because Olive *might* have skipped class; perhaps Mathilda had found out how great Pip was, Olive's very own flesh and blood; perhaps Mathilda also thought that their lives were like parallel lines that would – should – cross.

Mathilda pushed up her jumper sleeves. 'We just have to ask you something. Unless you're too busy planning that camping trip *with your father.*'

Mathilda laughed. Amelia laughed, too. Their laughs were as empty as the smiles of the rotating clown heads at the school fair. Olive wished she had balls to stuff down the Till–Mill throats and cursed herself for falling for them again. She stared at the corner of a leaf that was stuck to the underbelly of Mathilda's shoe and hoped that the leaf was stuck on with chewing gum, or the guts of some dead marsupial.

Amelia crossed her arms. 'What's a ho?' she asked.

Olive looked up from Mathilda's shoe and turned red.

'I told you she didn't know.' Mathilda looked at Amelia.

'I do too,' said Olive, more haughtily than she'd intended.

They both glared at her. *Man*, thought Olive, *where's Pip when you need her?*

Olive had no idea what to say. Ho was one of those words she definitely knew; she just didn't know what it actually meant – and she knew that she should. It was like not knowing what group sang what song on the radio (which Olive never did).

'So what is it?' Mathilda kicked Amelia.

'It's like . . .'

The two girls stared down at Olive. Their faces were black against the windows behind them. The gym was suddenly still.

'It's like, you know,' said Olive, looking to the stuck leaf for answers (which were not forthcoming). 'It's hard to explain. It's like, you know. Like . . . a skanky ho.' Olive held her breath until she thought she might just float up and away like an air balloon.

The talking around her started up again. The answer, although patently unsatisfactory, seemed to have satisfied Mathilda and Amelia, and laughing (definitely *at*, not *with*, Olive), they started a conversation about something else. Olive had been dismissed. She shuffled to the other side of the gym.

Olive leaned against the rock-climbing wall and blurred her eyes. She breathed in and tried to act like she didn't care. She took out her phone and scrolled through the numbers, hoping the other girls would think that she had heaps of friends, all of whom knew about hos and pop songs.

She got to the end of the list of names (MOG (W), MOG (M), TAXI) and then scrolled through them from the top again. She hooked her thumbs into the cuffs of her jumper and stared out of the window.

While Mog often commented on how fast time went when she was having fun, she had never commented on how devastatingly slow it could be when she was sad. Olive stretched her eyes open wide to stop the tears from slipping out. There was nothing left of her, nothing but tears and an emptiness like a hollow.

'Hey.'

Olive looked up.

'Want to come up here?' May was waving down at Olive from a tower of crash mats. She patted her hand on the blue plastic beside her. The gesture was so kind that Olive wanted to throw her arms around May. It felt like the single kindest thing that anyone had ever done for Olive: kinder than when Okey Doke threw in an extra flavour for nothing; kinder than when Mrs Graham added Olive's name to the Graham family height chart on their laundry wall.

Olive sniffed. 'Hi, May, thanks so much, that's really

nice of you,' she said and then felt silly. Olive hoped she hadn't looked like a desperado. Mog always said that nothing stinks like desperation.

May gave Olive a hand and hauled her up onto the mat. 'Don't be dumb.' From the pile of crash mats, they were higher than everybody.

May nodded in the direction of Amelia. 'Have you heard who's going to be Mary?'

'Oh, was Amelia replaced?' Olive inexplicably felt a bit bad. When she was first chosen, Amelia had made it pretty clear that she saw Mary as a springboard to a part on *Neighbours*. 'What part's Amelia playing now?'

May giggled. 'She's one of the four Doric columns holding up the stable roof.'

The columns were a bit pagan for a Christmas pageant, but they were left over from the school's Olympic opening ceremony. Year 7 had studied Greek columns in History, and even Nut Allergy could identify Dorics as the plainest of the columns.

'Apparently Amelia told Mrs Dalling that if she had to be a post, she wasn't settling for anything less than Corinthian,' said May. 'But it fell on deaf ears.'

Olive smiled. 'Who's the new Mary, then? They don't have much time to learn the role.'

'Maybe Skyep,' called a boarder with a face like a Knitting Nancy from the other side of May. Skyep's name wasn't really Skyep, it was Skye Parsons, but as there were four Skyes, each added the first letter of their surname to the end of the 'Skye' bit: Skyep, Skyeg, Skyet and Skyez.

Skyep was the newest girl in Year 7; she'd arrived mid-term from a state school. She was tall with a heart-shaped face, curvy breasts and a French manicure. She'd distinguished herself on the first day by wearing blue eyeliner.

'Common,' Mathilda had said at the time.

'Very sixties, actually,' Amelia had retorted. And from then on, to the extent that she had wanted to embrace it, Skyep was in.

'Skyep? Mary's going to another Year Seven?' May twirled an earring. 'Isn't she a bit new?'

The boarder with the face like a Knitting Nancy shrugged. Mary usually went to Year 9 establishment. Amelia had been an anomaly. And the part never went to a new girl, not even a popular one.

'It's going to be some Year Nine,' called another boarder. 'Stable-East said it can't go to anyone who wears make-up, even if the costume is a perfect fit.'

'Why do they always give Mary to the prettiest girls?' Olive piped up, then wished she hadn't. May and the Knitting Nancy looked at her, waiting for her to continue. Olive concentrated, forming her words cautiously. 'Well, nobody looks great in labour, and Mary's meant to be on the verge of giving birth. I doubt that she'd have had time to do her nails.'

This was something Mog had said about a television show last year, but Olive was happy to pass it off as her own. The other girls laughed. As she smiled with them, Olive felt herself growing taller and wider. The laughter sprang around the insides of the bigger Olive. She felt like a queen.

'What part are you playing?' May twirled one of the little gold baubles in her ears.

Olive shrugged. 'Townsperson forty-two or something.'

'Me too,' said May. 'Still, better a townsperson than a column.' Olive and May beat their legs against the mat. This time of year was nice; it was more relaxed, because most things had started to wind down for the long summer break.

'You might only be townsperson forty-two, but at least your folio has been hung.' May moved on to her other earring. 'It's the first thing people will see when they walk into the foyer.'

'Has it?' Olive smiled. She tried to look friendly but disinterested. On the inside, however, Olive was bubbling. She bit her lip to contain herself. 'Did yours get in, too?' Olive was a good drawer, but nobody could do cartoons like May.

'Nah. Your folio was the only one for Year Seven. Stable-East said mine will probably get up next year.' May smiled and began chatting to the boarder with the face like a Knitting Nancy about last night's lasagne. 'Broccoli? Broccoli? Who ever made lasagne with over-cooked broccoli?' asked May. 'At home they say even mince is for peasants.'

Olive excused herself and snuck out to the foyer.

23
A Hobbit,
But a Talented Hobbit

The parquet floor of the foyer was plaited; in the morning sun, it gleamed like school-fete toffee. Olive had long figured that the architect of the hall had taken a leaf out of *Hansel and Gretel* when she'd designed the building, because she'd filled it with lolly-like features to lure kids in.

Olive looked up. There on a board in the middle of the foyer was her painting, centre-front. It was a picture of a globe that was being whipped around by a gossip of girls. Their dresses blurred as the globe spun, but the countries had been painted precisely, and if you looked carefully (and in the right spot) you could even see snow on the peaks of the spinning Himalayas.

Olive was incredibly proud of it. It really did look like it was moving. She'd called it 'Confidence Makes the World Spin Round' while she'd painted it, but she hadn't had the confidence to call it anything out loud. Instead there was a tag that said, very grandly, OLIVE GARNAUT, 7C, UNTITLED.

The second piece was a linocut of Olive's home. Mog was gardening in the front yard. 'That is imaginative!' Mog had said when Olive told her about the picture.

The third was a sketch of Pip in pencil. Her shoulders were feathery, but her face was shaded and very detailed. Ms Stable-East had called it OLIVE GARNAUT, 7C, SELF-PORTRAIT.

'Can you believe they called that one "Olive"? It looks nothing like you,' said Pip. 'I was just trying to find a pen to change it. I mean, look at the hair. It's long! Even when yours was long, you didn't wear it in a loose pony-tail. And you never look straight at anyone like that. You talk to people's knees.'

'Thanks,' said Olive, but nothing could ruin this moment. She wanted to savour it. Mog might never see her work, but Olive wanted to keep living the time when her paintings were up there, centre-front.

'Well, you do talk to people's knees,' said Pip. 'Still, well done. It's just like in a proper gallery. Can I get your autograph?' Pip thumped her sister on the arm.

The bell rang and a bunch of Year 9s, as tall as Mog, burst in from the gym.

'Take them down, take them down! I don't want them to see.' Olive grated her nail along her bottom teeth.

'Olive, you're nuts. You were gloating twenty seconds ago.'

'That was with family, and I was not gloating.' At that

moment, Olive would rather have been back in front of Mathilda and Amelia than waiting for the approaching big girls. 'I love my pictures being here, but I don't want anyone to see them. I can't explain it.' Olive ducked behind the display board.

Pip followed. 'Don't worry about it. They're great, I promise.'

Olive put her index finger to her mouth in a desperate shush. The big girls were now directly in front of the display. Olive could see their racehorse calves under the board.

'Hey, check this out,' said one of the Year 9 girls. 'Can you believe that was done by a Year Seven?'

'Not bad,' said another.

'Olive Garnaut,' said a third, pronouncing it 'Gar-nort' instead of 'Gar-no'. 'Who's that?'

Olive froze. She felt sick. She waited for them to say, *Oh, that's the skinny runt with bee-sting boobs and no friends. A real Nut Allergy.*

'No idea.'

Olive bit down on her finger. One of the big girls shifted her weight from one foot to the other. There was silence for a second; the sort of silence that suggested the others probably shrugged.

'Cute blonde girl. Tiny. Sort of albino,' said one. 'In Burnett.'

'She looks like her self-portrait!' shrieked another, shrill with her own cleverness.

'A hobbit, but a talented hobbit.'

They all laughed.

'Hey, check out Tamsin's stuff,' called a girl further along the board, and the row of shaved legs and scuffed T-bars inched up to join her.

Olive flushed. Her blood soared. They liked her pictures. *They* liked them. The big girls thought *she* was talented. Olive Garnaut: talented *and* cute.

'Let's go to the tuckshop.' Pip took Olive's hand.

'No thanks, I'm going back to the gym.'

'Oh. Do you want anything? Cheesy roll?'

Olive shook her head.

'OK,' said Pip. 'It is a weird colour, anyway, that cheese.'

Olive smiled and, squeezing her art victory hard to her chest, she drifted back to find May and the boarder who looked just like a Knitting Nancy.

When the girls got home from school that afternoon, the electricity was still buzzing in Olive's bones. She lay in the bath and relaxed as her hips bobbed on the surface. Her hair floated out around her face like a lion's mane. Olive felt wonderful; she had an almost new friend and she was *talented*.

'Hey.' Pip strolled into the bathroom. Olive snapped up and hung her chin on the edge of the bath. She angled her body towards the wall. 'Pip, it's polite to knock.'

'Sorry, but we forgot something.'

'What?' asked Olive, convinced that nothing could destroy this day.

'Money,' said Pip, destroying it in one word.

Olive sighed. In all her euphoria, she had forgotten

that tomorrow was Thursday. D-Day. Well, W-Day – WilliamPetersMustardSeed-Day.

Pip sat on the edge of the bath. Olive groped for a flannel.

'Do we have to go tomorrow?' Olive drew the flannel over her face, breathing its distinctive soggy smell.

'Yes, we do. You promised.'

Olive frowned and twisted the flannel. She couldn't articulate her anxiety to Pip. She couldn't express that she was worried about seeing her father because she was scared that she'd evaporate; that to see him could mean being consumed by him. That he – that it all – felt too big. She was Olive Garnaut, daughter of Mog, sister of Pip, a hobbit but good at art. Despite all her imaginings, Mustard Seed was an unknown ingredient. He could rupture that.

'Maybe we can ask Mog for some money for a school excursion – say we're going to the zoo for Science or something.' Pip plucked the flannel from Olive's face, put it on the soap dish and passed Olive the phone. 'Go on, Ol. You can tell her about the exhibition, too.'

'Are you sure we can't do it in the holidays?' The discussion had bleached Olive's art display excitement.

'I'm sure. Mog might miss us then. We planned for tomorrow, so we should stick to it,' Pip said firmly. She pressed the talk button and Olive could hear the dial tone hammer. 'Besides, it's a good time because Mog will be out.'

Olive closed her eyes and saw Mog bubbling over a glass of wine and pesto with the Attorney-General while all the other parents bubbled over Olive's pictures at school. 'Pass me a hand towel.'

Pip smiled. 'So we're back on?'

Olive dialled Mog's number. Mog agreed to leave some money out on the bench later that night. 'Oooh, how fun. Make sure you get a photo of the white tiger for me. One of my clients was saying that the new enclosure is fantastic. Really realistic.'

Olive felt dreadful again. She wanted to tell Mog that the money wasn't for the zoo, but for WilliamPetersMustardSeed, whom she was travelling to see with *just* Pip on a school day, even though she knew Mog would be worried and livid and hurt, and that there was a real risk of Stranger Danger, even on a train; in fact rural Stranger Danger, which might just be worse.

But Olive caught Pip's eye and didn't say a word.

24
Upwardly Mobile

Early the next morning, Olive and Pip lay awake in bed waiting for Mog to leave. Olive breathed into the sheets and snuggled in the reflected warmth of her breath. The clock clicked forwards and Mog scrambled out the door. As soon as they heard it snip shut, Pip jumped up. 'Come on. Get dressed.'

'How is it that I have to drag you out of bed every morning for school, and you make me late anyway, but now, on a not-school day, you're up before the possums have gone to bed?'

Pip ignored Olive and bounced around the bedroom filling a rucksack with their supplies.

Olive buttoned her skirt. It was her favourite – navy with cream velvet trim. She looked up at Pip, who was strutting about the bedroom. 'You can't wear that!'

Pip had on a very short skirt, which she had teamed

with the *just like that* top and a pair of Mog's high heels. There was an inch of gap at the back of the shoes because her feet were too short and had slipped forwards.

Olive tucked in her shirt. 'Pip, we're going to meet our father. We should look like us. Besides, I thought it might be quite nice if we dressed the same – you know, like proper twins.'

Pip pulled a face and tugged the *just like that* top down over her shoulder. It dunked so low that Olive could see the skin on her chest, which had marbled in the cold.

'OK, I'll pick something else. I'm too chilly anyway. But I don't want to wear the same stuff. We do that every day, and it's geeky. Girls in middle school should not wear matching gear.' Pip looked at Olive's skirt. 'Please don't tell me you've got two of those . . .'

As Pip changed into a denim dress, Olive double-checked the provisions. She added the photo of Mog and the saffron-robed babies, together with a lovely picture of Mog on the front page of a law journal. She was in her wig and gown, shaking the Prime Minister's hand for being a woman and a successful barrister. In her heels, she had to bend her knees to reach him, but she looked slender and stylish and smiley. She looked a success.

Olive picked up the Brass Eye and tucked it in the front pocket of the rucksack.

'What are you bringing that for?' Pip did up her dress. 'You're not going to give it to him, are you?' She looked shocked.

'No. No of course not.' Olive zipped up the pocket and patted it twice. 'For joss.'

'Joss?'

'Luck.'

The twins walked into the kitchen to make breakfast. Instead of excursion money, Mog had left a note on the table, sticky with drops of butter and jam.

Ahhhhhhh! Tried three ATMs, but all were broken. What is it with banks? Here's a cheque. If there's a problem, tell them to stick it on the account. Isn't that what they usually do?

Have fun.

x Mog

P.S. Break a leg tonight – can't wait to hear all about it. Call me on the mob when it's over and you can join us.

Pip read the note and scrunched it up. 'Bugger. So much for joss.'

'She's right. They do always stick it on the account – I forgot. Guess we can't go.' Olive put the rucksack down.

'Don't be dumb, Ol. We have to go. We're all organized.'

Olive looked at her toes. Pip had managed to ladder her best socks. 'I don't know. I feel really uncomfortable about—'

'Olive Garnaut, you're a freak. You marched right up to the fake Mustard Seed without thinking, and *now* there's a problem?'

'I did not. I just didn't have time to think it thr—'

'For your information, this is not just about you,

Olive. This is *our* father. We have a right to know who he is, and if you don't want to go, I'll go by myself.'

Pip stared at Olive with a starched face. Olive looked at the clock. It wasn't even seven o'clock. They'd run out of time if they didn't leave soon, though. 'But what about money?'

'We've got about twenty-two dollars. We're taking food. If it's not enough, we can put the tickets on Visa – I don't think Mog's going to know. The statement won't say "two return tickets to Noglarrat". Look.' Pip picked up a statement that was on the bench and flapped it at Olive. It only listed the place of purchase and the relevant company. If Mog commented on the train company, they could say they'd bought tickets for school.

'OK, OK.' Olive sighed. In a way, she felt solid with Pip there. Pip was like a brace. No matter how big their father was, he could never consume Pip too. 'I'll go, but we'd better be quick. I want to be home before Mog is.'

Pip whooped as Olive collected the rucksack. Olive headed out of the front door with Pip at her heels.

The morning was wet and cool. The streets were as black and shiny as an oil slick. The twins picked their way between hamburger wrappers and discarded pickles flecked with sauce. They had even beaten the street cleaners.

The tram they had to catch wasn't difficult, as Olive had been on it before. It was even easier at this hour, because it was too early for the wise-crack schoolboys with tags scribbled all over their bags.

Olive walked towards the ticket machine. She could tell that Pip didn't want her to buy a ticket. It was *in-tu-ition* again, and Olive knew it as surely as she knew that Mog would throttle her if she found out what they were doing. She looked back at her sister and started poking coins in the slot. It wasn't worth the stress. Olive was stressed about enough things already without being caught by an inspector in disguise. Besides, they'd got sneaky lately. The girls at school said that they'd even started dressing up as students and knit-one-purl-one grannies. You just never knew where an inspector was going to spring from.

Olive poked another coin into the slot and thought of Macca, with her blue streaks and Birkenstocks. Ministers didn't look like ministers these days, and ticket inspectors didn't look like ticket inspectors. Life was all very tricky.

They arrived at the station to discover that the train had been delayed. By almost two hours. The girls camped in what was once the *Ladies Only* waiting room. Olive looked out of the window. The station was striped with grey-faced business people walking in lines.

Olive's phone buzzed to signal a text.

'Is that Mog already? It's only nine-thirty a.m. – I thought she only called at night.' The wait was making Pip jittery.

'She does, usually.' Olive trawled through the rucksack.

Pip paced the room. 'I hadn't thought about the phone. If Mog calls and it's on, she'll know where we are.

She'll only know later, when the bill comes in, but still . . .'

Olive clicked into the message. 'It's not Mog.'

Harriet the Spy. Ur not the only 1 who's gr8 with clues. We bet we no where uve gone & we're cumin 2.

'Who's it from?'

Olive shook her head. 'Who do you think? Why are they so awful?' She passed the phone to Pip, who dropped it. The mobile smacked the floor and noise exploded, bouncing around the metal *Ladies Only* roof. Neither of the girls moved.

'Do you think they're for real?' asked Olive.

'I don't know. Maybe you're right. Maybe we should just forget it. Wait until the holidays or something.'

Olive walked to the window and watched the platforms haemorrhage people. She couldn't see one single Joanne d'Arc blazer among them. She blew on the window and the suits dissolved in a mist.

'They won't come.' Olive shook her head.

'How do you know?'

'They won't. It's puff.'

'Look, Ol, they do have a track record of following through. Maybe we should leave it? They could really muck things up.'

'Pip, this is crazy! Three hours ago you were trying to convince *me*! They're just trying to intimidate us. They won't show.'

Pip clicked her tongue.

'They won't, Pip. They don't even know where we're going. How could they?'

'We know they *definitely* saw the map – in Maths that time – and we now know they *probably* nicked it.' Pip looked quite small sitting by herself on the long cream bench.

'We don't know that, Pip.'

'Did you ever find the copy?'

Olive stood up. 'No, I didn't find it, but I don't think we'd marked it. Anyway, if they were going to come, they'd be here already. I'm sure of it.'

Pip cocked her head to the side, then smiled. 'Well, I do know Mathilda won't come by herself. She can't do anything without asking Amelia.' She jumped up and held out her fist in a fake microphone. '*Now tell me, Mathilda, have you ever wiped your bottom without Amelia's permission?*' Pip flicked a pretend noodle ponytail. '*Hmmm . . . sometimes.*'

The girls were interrupted by the mobile, which broke into song on the floor, sucking the laughter out of the room.

'I'll get it.' Pip reached out for the phone.

'Leave it,' said Olive, picking up the mobile with two fingers as if it were radioactive. She held the 'off' button down until the screen turned blue and then blank. 'That should stop it.' The room was quiet.

'I can't believe you just did that.'

Olive tossed the phone into the top of her bag and grinned. 'I'm over them.'

25
Tripping Through the Garden State by Rail and Road

Thirty minutes later, the train to Noglarrat pulled away from the station. Olive watched as city buildings and cranes whipped past the window. 'We're off,' she said. 'We're actually off!'

The morning sun warmed her skin. Olive felt a surge of happiness and freedom that made her giddy.

Pip stuck her head out of the open window: 'Wheeeeeeeeeeeeeeeeeeeee.'

Olive didn't quite feel that free. 'Don't do that – your head might get lopped off.'

'C'mon, try it. It feels like flying. It feels loveleeeeeeeeeeeeeeeeeeeeeeeeee.' Pip's voice was picked up by the wind and blown along the tracks.

Olive stuck her head gingerly outside. The wind pulled her hair back and massaged her scalp. It did feel wonderful, even just a moment of it. Olive imagined that it felt exactly the same as driving in Amelia's father's GST convertible.

'Tickets!' The girls heard a thud as the door to the next compartment was opened.

'Crap, the inspector,' said Pip. The girls pulled their heads in. 'I'll disappear. Don't want to go drawing attention to ourselves. They'll be looking for two girls, not one.' She climbed up onto the luggage rack and crouched down behind the rucksack.

'What on earth are you doing?' Pip's head poked up over the top of the rucksack. Olive tried to pull her sister back down. 'We've got a ticket for you, and I swear if anything's going to draw attention to us, this will.' Pip could be so ridiculous.

'Tickets!' The door slid open. People in uniforms always made Olive feel nervous. She'd caught that anxiety from Mog. Mog wasn't scared of police, because she saw them in court and she said that they were usually trigger-happy young blokes who were as thick as planks. But Mog was very edgy around customs inspectors and sniffer dogs when they went on holiday. *They always make me feel like I might have a bag full of pastrami or some other forbidden product*, Mog would say (even though she was a committed vegetarian).

Olive worried, too, but not about pastrami. She'd seen *Bangkok Hilton*. She'd followed the Schapelle Corby case. Olive was terrified that somebody would plant drugs on her person.

'Ticket?'

'Oh, sorry.' Olive pulled the tickets they'd bought earlier that morning out of her wallet. This inspector wasn't interested in pastrami or discovering drugs on her person.

'Where are you off to?' he asked, clipping holes in her card. He had a dimple in his chin that sank as he spoke. It made his face twinkle.

'To see my father.' Olive's hands were sticky. The inspector nodded and dipped into his leather pouch. 'Want a balloon?'

'Um, thank you,' said Olive, too polite to mention that she was actually twelve.

'You can have one of these, too.' The inspector dipped deeper into his pouch and produced a chocolate Swiss roll.

'Yum, thanks,' said Olive, a little more genuinely. Swiss rolls were deliciously processed, soft and feather-light.

'Grab me one and ask if he's single,' hissed Pip from the luggage rack. The inspector, however, had already left, shutting the door behind him.

Olive pulled the sponge in two and handed half to Pip. The girls uncurled the Swiss roll. They dug the fake cream out with their fingers, saving the middle kernel until last. As they licked their hands they bickered and bantered, watching while never-ending cows in never-ending paddocks streamed by their window.

'This service will be pulling into Noglarrat in ten minutes. Please prepare to disembark,' boomed a tinny voice almost three hours later.

Olive stood up and stretched, then went to shut the window.

'Leave it open a smidge, can you? I'm a bit sick and the air's good for me.' Pip did look a bit green.

'That will teach you to eat so quickly. Want a peppermint? Mog says they help digestion.'

Pip shook her head. 'We ate hours ago. Besides, it isn't that kind of sick.'

'It's not your period, is it?' Olive lived in fear of getting her period, and in mortal fear of getting her period on public transport.

'No.'

The girls were quiet as the train click-clack-clacked over the tracks. Olive poked her sister's knee. 'You're not still worried about Amelia and Mathilda, are you? Because they won't—'

'No. It's more than them.' Pip chewed on her cuticle. 'What if he's awful, Ol? What if he's a Stranger-Danger stranger? These things don't always end happily.'

Olive sat back. Pip was scaring her.

Ever since Pip had first suggested finding Mustard Seed, Olive had lain awake in bed at night writing the story of the hunt for their father in her head. When she was positive – and she tried to be – the story ended with greasy chicken fingers and a bucket of KFC; but mostly it started with 'Once upon a time'. On these nights, the story had a musty spine and yellow pages that crackled, and it was filled with black woods and wolves and hunters and witches and lurking shadows and the smell of gunpowder and all the unaccountable creaks and thumps that old houses make only at night.

These stories had a distinctly Germanic feel, which meant that they would never, could never turn out well. Mog had told Olive that. At the end of the Second World War, when the Allies marched into Germany, the first thing they did, even before planting their victory flags, was pull the *Grimms' Fairy Tales* off the shelves, because they were too, well, grim.

In Germany, things didn't always work out with Bambi and a bluebird. That only happened in America. In the real world, Hansel and Gretel got eaten by the witch in a crunch of bones; eaten without so much as a thread of apron or a Hansel-burp to let their father know what had happened to his knock-kneed children. The real world was tough.

Olive didn't live in Germany, but she did live in the real world. She lived in a world where the lighthouse could be an oven, Mustard Seed a witch. He might have craggy nails and a starvation cage. He might be Stranger Danger – fathers weren't all good.

Sometimes, Mog came home distressed because she saw things in court. She saw fathers who had lost their children in divorces, and then committed unmentionable crimes. The worst thing was that these fathers looked normal. They had photos taken with white-zinced noses, spinning their kids round in the surf.

Fathers weren't always like Mr Graham or Mr Forster, and there could be just no saying what Mustard Seed would be like. All Olive knew was that at night, Mustard Seed got bigger and stronger and hairier and craggier, until he was part witch, part maniac, and only the teensy-weensy, inciest bit flaky hippy.

'We are now approaching Noglarrat station, where this service will be terminating. Thank you for travelling with Victorian Trains today.'

Olive looked at her sister and then at her watch – it was only just lunch time at the Joanne d'Arc School for Girls. She put her face to the window. Everything was yellow and dusty and seemed not only a million miles from school, but a million miles from a limestone light-house by the sea.

26
A Map for Living

Noglarrat station didn't have much to recommend it. It was an old station and its ironwork had been left to corrode in the weather like moth-gnawed lace. Everything looked tired except the vending machine, which blinked in the sun.

A boy in a fleece top, stooped in the corner, was the only person on the platform. He had a homemade cigarette, which flared as he drew back on it. 'Mornin',' he mumbled as the girls walked by. Olive walked faster.

'Spacey . . . two fancy girls,' he muttered, then collapsed to the ground in a tangle of limbs.

Pip stared. 'Where the bezoozus have you brought me?'

Olive pulled *Victorian Maps: Tripping Through the Garden State by Rail and Road* out of the rucksack and took a very deep breath. 'We've got a fair way to walk. We should probably get going.'

※ ※ ※

They found the mouth of the track without too much fuss.

'Just down there, past the dogleg,' said a woman at the milk bar, looking at the map. Her skin was as lumpy as barley soup. A short eyelash lay thick across the lens of her glasses, like a crack. She handed Olive a photo-copied map. 'This is probably a better one. Now, where are we?' She rubbed her glasses on her T-shirt. When she put them back on, the eyelash hadn't moved.

'OK, you're here.' She drew a slack star. 'Watch the track; only the first part is sealed.'

'Thanks.' Olive handed over coins for a bottle of water and tried not to touch the woman's skin.

The path was even longer than Olive had predicted. The first part was easy, but once the tarmac ended, the sand fell away under their feet.

'This feels like army training.' Pip's face was red.

'When have you ever trained for the army?' Olive was holding her arms up to shade her face and they were getting tired. The sun was stingy. They walked along the edge of the track, trying to catch the tea-tree shadows.

'Stick to the grass bits,' said Olive. 'It sort of anchors the sand.'

'Shouldn't we be dropping bread, like Hansel and Gretel? Or pebbles?' Pip shucked leaves from an over-hanging branch.

'Look at that,' said Olive. They were passing a rock. Somebody had sprayed a slogan across its mossy front.

'Sounds like Mog's "chaos is order waiting to be decoded" crap,' said Pip.

Olive laughed. 'It's funny, chaos. When I was little, I caught a taxi into the city every Friday afternoon with Sarah Afar.'

'The babysitter you hated? The role-player?'

Olive rolled her eyes. 'Yep. That's the one. Anyway, Sarah Afar was practising for some obsessive-compulsive role. Every Friday we'd leave school to see Mog at 3.17 p.m. – just after the bell. Sarah Afar would have the taxi waiting. She'd direct the driver along the same route, and we'd get every single green light.'

'What if there were roadworks, or an accident?'

'Not then – but if we went the same way, on a normal day, we really would get every green light except the one just before Chambers. That would always be red, and then we'd get out.'

'That is weird.'

'I'd forgotten about it.'

'Did Sarah Afar say anything?'

'Yep, she'd say, "There's order in everything," and then she'd dump me with Mog's secretary, put the money-envelope in her handbag, and pat it twice just to make sure it was there.'

Pip and Olive continued along the track, walking and talking in time. As they walked, Olive thought the Sarah Afar story through. While the streets had heaps of people and cars, there was a pattern to the mess. It seemed there was a map for living that just hadn't been drawn up yet. Mog *would* like that.

After miles of track and many water stops, the path finally spread out.

There, at the end, was a lighthouse.

It was bigger than it had looked in Mog's picture. Bigger and grittier: a vast, greying tower gripping the edge of its cliff. The lighthouse was girt by grass, tough and barbed, growing in patches like a dog's mange. Despite the sun, the wind was cold.

'The sea mist didn't look this clammy in the picture,' said Olive, pulling on her cardigan.

'You couldn't see the sand mites, either.'

The wind bellowed up over the rock face. Olive clamped her teeth. She tried to imagine Mog there, but she couldn't. The place was uncontained, and it somehow felt nasty. The ground trembled as waves punched the cliff. It couldn't really be *the* lighthouse.

'Look.' Pip pointed to a van set in the tea-tree scrub. The van was orange but bleached – the colour of dusty vitamin C pills in a bottle (rather than the tablets, which bled scarlet under Olive's tongue). It was rusted right through in patches, and light fell across its remaining seats in bands, like crochet.

The twins approached the van.

'It's full of dirt.' Pip picked up a splinter of eggshell and held it out to Olive. 'It smells like the sea.'

'It smells like chicken poo,' said Olive. Somebody had

strung wire across the gap where the door should have been – a few feathers quivered in it.

Pip slid her hand down the gap and fished around with her fingers. She pulled out a badge with a pop and a shower of chicken pellets. Pip rubbed the button and pinned it on her sister's top: HAWKE CRIED BECAUSE HE LIED. 'Who was Hawke again? Was he the Prime Minister who drowned – the one they named the swimming pool after?'

Olive giggled, nervy. 'They should've gone for a life-saving club, but that wasn't him. Hawke's the Prime Minister who was in *The Guinness Book of Records* for drinking the most beer.'

Olive tried to take the badge off, but her hand was trembling and the catch was stuck.

Pip pointed at the handle of a teaspoon jammed in the ignition and then circled the van. 'EIO 222 – it's definitely the same as the one in the photo.'

Olive kicked an old bottle lying on the ground. It rolled slowly. 'Come on,' she said, motioning at the light-house. 'Let's go inside.'

The girls reached the door and stopped. The tower loomed above them, immense and unforgiving.

'This place is like freaksville.' Pip was whispering even though there was nobody in sight. 'If we died out here, it would take them forty years to find our bones.'

Olive took a shaky breath. She tapped on the door. The wood was crumbly in places, and it smelled sour. There was no answer. She knocked a bit harder, in the middle. Nothing. She gave the door one last beat. The wind snarled and the door scraped open.

Olive and Pip stepped inside. The air was thick and damp and smelled like pumpernickel. Olive stood still, trying to suppress her heartbeats while she waited for her eyes to adjust. Once the light had bent and warped and then settled, she saw that she was in the pit of the tower. Some tiny windows high above illuminated things slightly, but the grainy gloom left Olive feeling like she was floating.

In all her imagining, Olive hadn't considered that the belly of the lighthouse would be as dank as compost.

'Hello?' Olive pitched into the silence. 'Hello?'

Olive breathed through her teeth to block the pumpernickel smell. A feral wind blustered in and rattled stale air and papers. The roof moaned. Olive crossed her arms into her cardigan and stared at an old beanbag dribbling grey beans onto the floor.

A staircase rose in a spindly tower from the centre of the room, like a great pile of pick-up-sticks, balancing, despite the odds, all the way to the speck windows above. Somebody had lined rings of empty whisky bottles around the base.

'I'm going to go up. Do you want to come?' Olive turned to see Pip edging back to the door.

'Let's not worry about it, Ol. I've seen enough.'

Olive's stomach fluttered. While she wanted to leave, desperately wanted to leave, she'd feel empty if she did.

Pip was standing in the doorway looking at Olive. 'I won't think worse of you if we go.'

Olive turned and readjusted the rucksack. 'Yes you

will. But that's not it. I need to. Let's just get this over.'

Pip raised her hand and stepped back out into the light. 'I'll keep guard, but call if you need me, and I'll . . . I'll think of something.'

Olive moved some of the bottles to the side and started to climb. The steps were smothered in a mesh of rubbish as layered as decoupage; they shifted in step with her feet. The metal had rusted in parts, leaving toothed edges, and Olive had to haul herself up along the banister to avoid the steps' bite. She imagined centuries of light-house keepers climbing those very stairs, to keep watch over whatever lighthouse keepers watched – rocks and ships and mermaids with breasts to lure sailors to their death – tackling the very same obstacle course with no company other than a ham sandwich.

As Olive climbed, the tower pressed in until the walls were so close she could see chiselled gouges in the stone. She climbed until her legs were wobbly and everything was lit with hoary light. She climbed until she reached a room.

The room was rimmed by a bench broken only by the stairwell. Windows filled with grey-day sea ran in a loop. Pieces of card had been taped over spots where the glass was broken. A clump of mauve fabric vibrated against a windowpane, rigid with salt and wind.

The lighthouse was empty. Quite empty. He had gone after all.

Olive watched through the windows as waves mauled hidden rock platforms below. She could feel herself beginning to extract from the situation. She could no longer smell dust or pumpernickel. She could barely feel the floor beneath her feet.

Neither of the girls had stopped to consider that Mustard Seed might not be there. It was dumb, really, but after the fake Mustard Seed incident, getting the right person and the right place had seemed like the entire battle. They had spent so long trying to figure out which lighthouse he lived in, and how and when to go there, and what he'd be *like*, that they'd managed to forget that he might have moved on.

Now they would get expelled from school for nothing – they hadn't even seen their father.

'Are you all right?' Pip called up the tower. Olive pulled the clump of fabric from the window and slowly descended the stairs. She listened to her steps bristle down the tower's spine.

'Was there anything there?' Pip had climbed up a few steps to meet her. She was standing on a heap of fraying hessian.

'Nope. The lighthouse has been adverse possessed by empty bottles. Empty bottles and this.' Olive held up the clump of mauve fabric. 'An old sari.'

Pip poked the crusty material with a finger. 'Oh,' she said quietly.

The girls stood on the steps and took in the scraps of a lost life.

'Come on, Ol. Let's get out of here.'

They wandered back to the mouth of the sandy path, in silence.

27
The Hon. and the SAG

Pip and Olive drooped over the milk bar counter. Olive ordered salad sandwiches, not because they particularly wanted salad sandwiches, but because it was too hot for pies and the only other option was curried egg.

When they came, the sandwiches had splotches that were beetroot-pink and soggy. The woman lumbered behind the counter squirting blue-heaven syrup, the colour of gel toothpaste, into a silver cup.

'So, how was the lighthouse then? You find it?'

'Yep.' Olive took a bite of sandwich. There was something comforting about the texture of margarine, white bread and lettuce.

'And how was it?'

'Empty.'

'I told you there wasn't much down there.'

No you didn't, thought Olive. *You didn't mention it.* Her feet were tired and she blamed the woman, even if the woman was thwacking generous blue-white balls of ice cream into their milkshake.

The woman didn't notice Olive's irritation. 'The government got rid of the squatters. They'd been there for years – used to be a bit of a hippy commune. Mainly student types, but they did add a bit of light and colour to the district. Now they're turning it into a B&B or something.'

'Oh.' Olive wished this were a discussion they'd had before she walked through the skin on her heels. 'Do you know a man called Mustard Seed? Did he live there?'

'Mustard Seed?' The woman jiggled the cup onto the blender. Skin flapped about her buttery elbows. 'Well, that's a daft name if I ever heard one. No man called that in Noglarrat. Lots of Gregs and Daves and Lleytons. Three babies in the last fortnight, all boys and all Lleytons. You wouldn't read about it.'

Olive looked away, her closed mouth distorted by a yawn. Fatigue was starting to smother her interest in locating their father.

'What about William Peters. Is there a William Peters . . .' Pip's voice didn't have the strength to lift for the question.

'You mean Bill Peters? We certainly do have a Bill Peters. He's our greatest SAG.'

The girls sat up.

'SNAG,' grunted a man Olive hadn't noticed, from behind a racing guide. 'Sensitive New-Age Guy, not a drooping sofa.' Something a bit crusty, probably egg, was dribbled down his T-shirt.

'SNAG, SAG, Bill Peters is Noglarrat's First Man, our Jackie O.'

Olive looked blank.

'He's married to Pat Peters, the Mayor. Got her sights set on Tidy Town for next year, she does. He's more of the arty sort.'

'Do they live here? In town?' Pip was leaning forwards over the counter.

'Of course they do. Fancy house in Christowell Avenue – oldest street in these parts. Here you go.' The woman wiped her hands across the front of her grease-stained apron. 'That'll be eight-fifty, love.'

Olive took the drink and walked outside. She had to suck hard to work the ice cream up through the straw. 'Bill Peters. Well, I guess that's him.' It was such a mousy, unadventurous name. 'I can't believe he's here after all.'

'I can't believe he lives in a house.' Pip's voice curled with contempt. 'Not even somewhere interesting like an old scout hall or a converted chocolate factory. How the mighty fall.'

Olive couldn't respond. She just felt hot and dusty and punctured.

The girls found Christowell Avenue on the photo-copied map and set off. It wasn't far. Nothing was far in Noglarrat, it seemed, except the lighthouse.

'Look.' Pip gestured up at a poster.

PAT PETERS

TAKING THE 'RAT' OUT OF NOGLAR-RAT.

YOUR LOCAL GOVERNMENT – WORKING FOR A SAFER,

TIDIER TOWN.

A woman with lacquered hair and a rubbish bag smiled out from the sign. Pat Peters. Mayor of Noglarrat. Mustard Seed's wife.

'Can my spam. *That's* her?'

Olive looked at the blunt edge of Pat Peters's shirt pleat. 'I don't think she knows she's married to a man formerly known as Mustard Seed.' Everything about Pat Peters seemed terrifyingly no-nonsense. She didn't look like the sort of woman to tolerate bongo drums, people sleeping in abandoned lighthouses or anything frivolous like gluten-free food.

'She can't have any idea.' Pip tilted her head to the side. 'I bet she's the type of person who would only let kids have one spread on their sandwiches – jam *or* peanut butter, never jam *and* peanut butter.'

Olive had to agree.

Behind the poster stretched Christowell Avenue. It was a shady street lined with trees. Each tree had a copper plaque, marking the name of a dead soldier who had fought a war in another time and hemisphere. The houses had gardens filled with bony geraniums, hoses that curled like green tapeworms, and lawns that had yellowed off to purple in the heat.

'How are we going to know which one it is?' Olive asked.

'Easy.' Pip pulled at a bundle of post peeping from a letterbox and held up an envelope. 'Mr and Mrs J. Phillips. We know Mustard Seed is not at number four.'

'And that Mr and Mrs J. Phillips have an overdue gas bill,' added Olive.

They laughed and walked on. 'Mr J. Anderson Esq. Not at number six, either.'

'Or number eight . . . or ten.'

The girls stopped in front of a house with a scrubbed fence too tall to peek over.

'*The Hon. P. and Mr W. Peters*. Number twelve.' Olive's voice stuck.

'What's with the "Hon."?' Pip giggled as Olive slid the envelope back into the silver slit of the letterbox.

'Honourable – for being the Mayor,' snapped Olive. 'This is it.'

Olive pressed her face to the gate and looked through its metal slats towards the house. The house was the same shape as the other bungalows in the street, only it had been iced in white paint until it had the patina of wedding cake. Ash-coloured pebbles were raked into sharp lines where there should have been grass. A waxed station wagon was parked in the open garage, a pine-tree air-freshener dangling under its mirror.

Olive started. Next to the car were six bikes, linked by a chain. The bikes were all different sizes but all blue, leaning in a row from tallest to smallest: an unravelled Russian doll.

'They've got . . . they've got children?' she whispered.

'They certainly do.'

Olive turned. A woman with a handful of cuttings was collecting a bin. She smiled.

'Two girls, two boys, as regular as knitting. You never saw such pretty babies.'

'No,' said Olive. 'I don't suppose I have.'

'Bill minds them – he's one of those stay-at-home dads. Give the gate a good hard shove; it can stick a bit in the heat.'

'Thank you,' said Olive as the bin rattled over the concrete.

Olive leaned her cheek against the cool of the gate.

Pip whistled air through her teeth. 'Four children. What's with that?'

Four children. Olive had been so caught up in all the extraordinary things Mustard Seed could be and the fact that he was her father, their father, that she hadn't imagined him as anybody else's.

She pictured his children now – the You Never Saw Such Pretty Children children – in a line like the von Trapp family from *The Sound of Music*, children in sailor suits with knickerbockers, rosy cheeks, and eyelashes as thick and dark as Amelia's. A family of curls and dimples. Imagining Bill Peters and his von Trapp family made Olive feel smaller, skinnier, sallower and totally unlovable.

'I guess we should get this over with, Ol.'

Olive shoved the gate open. 'It's all right, Pip,' she said slowly. 'I'll do this.'

Pip looked up at the house. 'Are you sure?'

Olive nodded.

Pip thumped Olive twice on her back – *chop chop*. 'OK, well, I'll meet you back at the poster.'

Olive watched Pip scuttle back towards the gate like a freed crab. At the end of the path, Pip paused and turned. 'I can't believe a father of ours has air-freshener.' She wrinkled her nose and slipped out onto the dead-soldier street.

28
Edges That Would Never Be Straight

Olive walked up the path with the reluctance of a first-day student. She wished that Mustard Seed lived in the lighthouse after all – not in a house like this, a house with all the warmth of shop-bought cake. The lighthouse might have been scary and tumbledown, but at least it was connected to Mog. This place was not.

Olive smoothed her hair behind her ears with both hands. She rang the doorbell. There was a pause and then a scramble of feet.

'Dad, Dad, there's someone here,' something cheeped.

The door was opened by two children, hazy through the security screen.

Olive swallowed. 'Um, hi. Is William Peters there, please?' His name tripped on her tongue, and she wondered whether it would ever be creamy.

'That's our dad.'

'Oh.' Olive didn't know where to look. Speaking to the flywire was like speaking to someone blind, someone with boiled-egg eyes. One of the children pressed a nose to the screen, and skin mulched through the holes in the mesh. Another two children emerged; they were blooming like bacteria.

'Dad, Dad.'

The lock was unsnibbed and the door pushed open.

Olive stared. The children were a knot of plump limbs, swimsuits, dark eyes and macaroni necklaces threaded on blue string. They looked thick and wholesome – as if they might just taste of butterscotch. They looked too soft for a shop-bought house.

Olive peered down the hall behind them, trying to take in as much of everything as she could, to sift through later. The house was catalogue-bare, with a spiky rug. An enormous picture of white-slash flowers in scratchy paint hung on the wall near the door.

One of the pretty-as-knitting kids puffed out her chest. 'Dad's making us currant muffins. You can have one if you like, when they come out of the oven.' She twirled a piece of macaroni at her throat.

'Excuse me, excuse me.' A man elbowed through the children to the door, wiping white-flour hands on a block-print sarong. His shirt was open and his skin was deep brown, but it wasn't smooth like Mr Forster's – it was thick and spotted. Dark hair swayed about his face and shoulders. Olive found herself staring straight into the black hooded eyes of her father.

'Are . . . are you William Peters?' she asked, although

instinctively she knew that he was. Her guts clenched.

The man squinted. 'Who are you?'

'Olive,' said Olive, remembering her name and her manners. She looked down and picked at a fleck of dried seaweed on her cardigan. 'You are, aren't you? You're William Peters.'

'Bill Peters, mainly.' There was an M crimped between his eyebrows. He took a step in front of his children, rearranging them behind his sarong. 'Can I help you?' His voice was textured, as if he'd just woken.

Olive smiled – not a full-teeth smile, but definitely more of a smile than a nod. She knew that her first proper thoughts should have been *My long-lost father sounds like me; my long-lost father looks like me; my long-lost father loves me the best of all these kids, and I love him truly and deeply already.*

She found, however, that she thought nothing of the kind. *My long-lost father wears a skirt*, thought Olive as she stared at the block-print fabric knotted on his hip. *My long-lost father has swinging hair and wears a sarong like women in the tropics.* She pictured Pip's face when she heard about this and bit down to plug a laugh.

WilliamPetersMustardSeed's tan had taken on a rosy sheen. His eyes narrowed when he saw the badge on her lapel. 'I'm sorry, but who are you?'

'Olive *Garnaut*,' said Olive clearly, hoping to clarify matters. 'Mog's daught—'

'Emily, Sophie, to your rooms to get changed, please. You know Mum hates wet togs inside – hang them up on their hooks in the laundry. Sam, could you have a look at the muffins? If they're ready, just one each please – don't spoil your dinner.'

The children filtered away.

'Whose daughter?' Mustard Seed's voice was tightly sprung.

'Mog Garnaut's.'

'Garo?' His mouth puckered at the point where the word dug.

'Garnaut. *Gar-no*.'

'Yes.' He turned and straightened the white-slash painting. There was silence – a silence so still that Olive could hear it. She stepped towards him. 'Don't you remember Mog?'

'No.' Something loosened in his throat. 'No, I'm sorry. I don't.'

'But you must remember her. Mog. Mog and the vegetable patch and the cake-fork van.'

'It doesn't ring a bell.' Mustard Seed had stiffened. Everything he did signalled that he was uncomfortable. Everything he did signalled that he was lying.

'Look, I'm sorry but I'm actually busy. I have four kids, Christmas is around the corner, and I haven't wrapped a single present. I'm really sorry, mate, but I have to go.'

The word *mate* cut through the air like a tomahawk. A blush shot up Olive's neck. She dug into the rucksack, trying to stop her eyes from getting watery. Dads didn't call their daughters *mate*. They called them 'princess' or 'angel' or 'sweet pea'.

Olive sniffed and pulled out one of the photos. 'You

must recall it. You just must. You washed me in the sea and cuddled me while we swung to drums by the fire; brown as berries and swinging free.' She held the picture out to him. 'See, here we are. The lighthouse, me and Mog and . . .'

Olive pointed to it so that William Peters or Mustard Seed or whatever he was called could remember.

There was no drum in the photo, no bathing in the sea, no WilliamPetersMustardSeed. She crunched her toes down hard. Olive hated being tripped up by her own dreamings.

Mustard Seed's face jumped when he saw the photo, and another silence shuffled about the porch. Olive pushed the photo right up to his head so he couldn't escape.

'Do. You. Remember. Mog.' Olive was firm, each word a separate sentence.

Mustard Seed sagged; his hands slunk to his sides.

'Of course I do.'

She looked up into the beaten face of her father.

One of the butterscotch children reappeared at the door. 'Dad, who is that kid?'

'Nobody, sweetheart. Just a girl collecting for charity. Fetch my wallet, will you?'

Mustard Seed's demeanour had changed upon the arrival of his daughter. His gestures were now extravagant, friendly, high-fiving bold. He looked at Olive: it was a look to mute.

Hurt shot up through Olive, from some cavern deep

in her gut. She bit the inside of her mouth to try to anchor it; control it. She couldn't.

'Nobody?' she asked. She could feel her anger pushing out. 'I'm *nobody*? Don't you even want to know what grade I'm in? Who my teacher is? How I've been?' Her shouts were exaggerated by the silence that trailed them.

Mustard Seed tightened the knot in his sarong. His shirt was starting to darken in bands under the arms. 'Emmie, fetch the wallet for Daddy, please.'

'But—'

'Now.'

He watched Emily pad off down the hall and turned. 'Look, I've got the kids to consider, and Pat. She'd kill me – she's the Mayor, you know.' He shook his head. 'It just can't be.'

But it can be, it can be, Olive wanted to beg. She could fit in there. She could help him with the kids. She was good at muffins. She'd spent years pulling them from the Grahams' oven. In fact, she'd been in training for this very moment.

Mustard Seed crossed his arms. His voice was quiet but muscular. 'No. It can't be. The kids have their needs.'

Olive shrank. She reached for her photo and flattened its bent ends against her top. There was in his words the smugness of a high-fenced family life, with drawings taped on the fridge, and pine-tree-shaped air-fresheners, and mountains of macaroni necklaces, and no room, no room for any more. There was a completeness about him, about his family. Everything in Bill Peters's life already had its spot.

216

'Here you go,' said the little kid called Emily as she skipped back up the hall dragging a bag.

'Thanks, Emmie. Go and help Sambo keep an eye on the muffins, will you? I'll just fix up here.'

'I'll pay, I'll pay.'

'OK then. You can help.' He looked at Olive and ladled the child up in his arms. 'Emily's our baby girl.' The child was too big to be a baby, but little enough to be held. She looped her arms around her father's neck.

Mustard Seed flipped his wallet open with his free hand, took out a twenty-dollar note and passed it to the little girl.

She shook her head. 'No no no. *I'll* do it! Only golden coins.'

'OK then.' Mustard Seed held out his wallet and she took a fistful of coins.

'One, two . . . three.' The little girl counted them out for Olive.

Olive took the money, but she couldn't look at the little girl; she couldn't look at her shining pigtails with their salted tips, couldn't look at her hand with its smudged star stamp.

'Oh well, goodbye then,' Olive mumbled. The words were too clumsy for everything they conveyed. She turned and walked; turned and walked with her head held high, with clipped-step poise: a walk to stop things from spilling. Her future stretched out before her, empty and wild, enormous and unchartered. *The kids have their needs. The kids have their needs. The kids have their needs.*

But I have them, too.

The door closed. Behind it, Olive could hear the child twittering, her voice amplified by the hardwood floor. 'She was a bit rude, Dad. She didn't even say thank you.'

Olive had reached the gate when the security door scraped. Mustard Seed came running behind her. He fished a pile of notes from his wallet. 'Look, how much do you need? Ten? Twenty? How much is a cab? You're not living here, are you?'

'No. Still Melbourne. We live in Melbourne.'

'Oh. Well . . .' He waved a clutch of money at her. 'Well, here you go, Olivia.'

'It's—' Olive's eyes fogged. 'It's—' She spun away from the notes, pushed the gate, then paused. She turned, lifted her chin and looked straight into Mustard Seed's black hooded eyes. 'I'm Olive, just Olive. Olive *Garnaut*.'

Olive ran down the street, towards Pip. Mustard Seed stood at the gate and piped words behind her in layers – nothing-words in a broken tone that nipped:

'Oh, Olive.

'Of course you're just Olive.

'Look, look . . .

'Um.

'Oh, I'm . . .

'Perhaps we could rustle up a fold-up bed . . .'

But the words didn't stop her.

Only once Olive had reached the end of his street did she pause. She took a deep breath of air and swung, giddy. She could feel Pip at her side.

'I had twelve years of questions, and I think you just

answered each one of them, you Mustard Moron,' Pip bellowed over the snarl of the traffic.

Olive rested her head against her sister's shoulder. It smelled safe; it smelled like Olive. She turned and vomited.

'Get up, Ol, quick. We've gotta get out of here.'

Olive's throat burned. Little bits of lettuce stung in her nose and stuck to her shoe. 'It's funny,' she said, wiping her mouth on the back of her hand. 'You expect the worst. You can't let yourself think that he might really be good, that he might really care. You think that sort of thing happens to other kids; that you don't deserve it; that you might jinx it if you think anything else – but somehow you jinx it anyway. And no matter how much you protect yourself, you feel so, well . . .'

'Try not to . . .'

'But you play games with yourself, Pip. You say, "If I do all my maths, if I use matching pegs on the line, if I sit at the deep end of the bath, it will work out." And you do those things, and it still doesn't.'

'You could sit in the deep end of the bath from now until you're a waterlogged granny, and nothing would change.'

Olive sniffed. 'I know. He'd still be blaming Pat Peters and his kids.'

Pip nodded. 'Anyway, family is the people you love. Blood counts for nothing.'

They walked back to the train station. Olive sat on the ground of the platform. Tears blistered. She could smell bile on her party skirt, in her fringe. The corner of the handmade frame poked out of the top of the rucksack. Olive pushed it back in. 'The edges aren't straight. I wanted it perfect.'

Olive leaned her head against the wall behind her. The evening shadows that climbed the station were almost as long and thin as the train tracks themselves. Olive was exhausted, but she was also sad; a plain gnawing sadness that was impossible to contemplate. She was sad for so many things – for Pip, for Mog, for herself – but mostly Olive felt sad for edges that would never be straight.

The essence from the tea-trees leached into the air as they excreted the last of the day's heat. The girls sat in a silence that was as snug and comfortable as Mathilda's Ugg boots.

'Ministers don't look like ministers these days, ticket inspectors don't look like ticket inspectors, hippies don't look like hippies, and dads don't look like dads,' said Olive.

The ground trembled as the 6.42 train to Melbourne approached.

'Well, ours certainly didn't act like one.' Pip stood up and stretched. 'C'mon, Ol, let's get out of here. Let's go home.'

29
Daughters of Mog

The trip back from Noglarrat felt quicker than the trip there. There was no sound but the beat of the carriage on the track. There just wasn't anything left to say. It was as if all the ideas, chatter and natter had drained away, and the only thing Olive had left was a headache hard in her forehead.

Pip lay on one of the seats and slept, the denim jacket bound around her face. Olive pressed her temples and studied her reflection in the window. She may have looked sepia in the train light, but she was Mog Garnaut's daughter, all right. She had come to find her father, but she had ended up finding Mog. There was nothing of Bill Peters, not one bit.

It was hard to tell if there was more of Bill Peters in Pip. Not only because she was currently encased in denim, but because her reflection was translucent. In the window, Pip had thinned, and all that was left were the lights from country towns flicking inside her silhouette.

Olive let her face sink into the window. She breathed in the cool from the glass and rocked with the carriage.

30
Silvery Moon

Three hours later, Olive sat in a taxi at the end of her street. The taxi driver punched his meter. 'Are you sure this is all right? There's not a lot round here.'

'Yes, thanks, I just live down there.' Olive didn't speak to the man, but to the ID on his dashboard.

'Well, OK then. Take care.'

The car drove off, leaving the road cold and silent. Olive stood under the dusky orange of a streetlight, looking at the photograph in her hand. In it, Mog squinted out from the vegetable patch with her peeling shoulders and an armful of saffron robes.

She was holding one pale baby.

Pip had vanished.

Olive ran towards the beach, tripping over knobs in the asphalt and cans in the gutter, her shoes *thwack thwack* on the pavement. Three workmen were digging a hole in the footpath under a spotlight. One whistled as she passed. Olive didn't care. She dropped down over the bluestone wall onto the beach. Her knee hit her chin as she landed, and her mouth bubbled thick with saliva and salt. Olive spat blood, wiped her mouth on the back of her sleeve, and pressed on, even though the sand grabbed her calves and ankles. She didn't stop until she got to the pier.

There was nothing left of the carnival but a bleached carton of Double Yoke Eggnog. Olive booted it to the water's edge, where the sand was sleek. She fumbled in her rucksack for the Brass Eye and ran into the sea.

Olive kicked at the waves, dragging her feet through the shallows, feeling her socks expand, heavy with brine. She pushed against the current, pushing and calling Pip's name, pushing even though her *in-tu-ition* told her it was useless.

When the tide tugged at Olive's hem, she knelt. Her lungs ached. The waves wove around her, washing cool across her lap; her skirt ballooned like leavened dough. Olive raised the Brass Eye to her face, shaking. But it was too dark; the Brass Eye was filled with shadows.

Olive lowered the cylinder to her cheek and listened to boats bump about their moorings. Behind her, the beach smouldered in the nightlights; before her, the sea sloshed metallic under the moon. She breathed in the fishy damp and, for just a few seconds, in the slip of silence between the knocking hulls, the water looked like a mirror – a flickering mirror of molten silver, liquid crystal and glass.

31
Lost and Found

Olive walked home with squelchy shoes and puckered fingers. Wet sand chafed her legs like facial scrub. She stepped over Pip's name imprinted in the concrete; before her, the house blazed.

As Olive let herself in the front door, Mog clacked across the hall in high heels. When she saw Olive, her face went sloppy. 'I thought I heard you.' She threw her arms around Olive and gripped her. 'Where on earth have you been?'

'Sorry.'

Mog ran her hands up and down Olive's arms, clutching at them as if she were rock climbing. 'Everything intact? You're wet.'

'Careful, Mog, that hurts.'

The grip slackened, but only faintly. '*Gott sei Dank*.'

While Mrs Graham spoke Spanish when she was

cross, Mog spoke German when she was relieved.

'Where did you go, Ol? With whom? I've got a massive search party combing every inch of Port Fairy. I've called all the hospitals. We've been looking for hours.'

Olive snatched her arms back. 'Why Port Fairy?'

'Mathilda rang me at work. She was worried because you weren't at school, and she was sure you'd gone there.'

'Mathilda?' Olive scrunched her face. 'That girl needs a hobby.'

Mog's laugh was gluey with tears.

'I wasn't at Port Fairy.'

Mog sucked deeply on her cigarette. 'Where – Jesus, Ol, I thought I'd lost you.' She squeezed her daughter and tapped her bottom. 'I'm tempted to have one of those council chips injected into your rump – then at least I'd be able to scan and locate you.'

Olive smiled. 'I thought you said those pet things were barbaric carcinogens.'

'*Effective* barbaric carcinogens.' Mog exhaled and smoke spread out in a fan over Olive's shoulder.

'You're the one who hasn't been around, Mog. Maybe I'll have one injected in you.'

Mog took Olive's arm and drew her into the morning room, where she stubbed out her cigarette on the rim of an empty vase. Then she pulled Olive to her chest again and stroked her hair. 'Where did you go?' Mog repeated. She rested her chin on her daughter's head.

'Away.'

Mog looked at Olive, head on a tilt. Her face was tired

without lipstick. 'Away where? It's after eleven. No Year Seven has the Freedom of the City, Olive, even one with a mother on a Big Case. It was just awful to discover news of my only child through her friends.'

Olive studied a leaf-shaped stain on the ceiling and shook her head. 'It's awful to discover news of your father through his children.'

'Father?' A crack slid about Mog's face. She ran her finger over the HAWKE CRIED BECAUSE HE LIED pin on Olive's cardigan and stiffened. 'You've seen him, haven't you?'

Olive nodded and whimpered. She had only a vague memory of black hooded eyes, a painting of slashes and a thatch of butterscotch limbs; these details felt so remote, they were no longer real.

'Why did you lie?' Mog's voice was taut.

Olive didn't answer. She really didn't know.

'How?' Mog took a breath. 'How did you find him?' She grated her chin along her daughter's parting and held her. 'Oh, Ol, why didn't you trust me? He's hopeless. Just hopeless.'

Olive looked up at her mother. 'I don't think he is.'

Mog flinched.

'Not hopeless.'

There was a silence long enough to count twelve of Mog's breaths.

'I just don't think there's room for me. He lives in the town now, with a wife and the . . . the children.'

'Oh,' said Mog, with an 'Oh' that could never be light. She breathed in Olive like she breathed in smoke. Then she whispered into Olive's scalp, so quietly that later Olive would wonder whether she had heard it at all, 'Nothing can ever replace a child, Ol. What great bloody fool would miss out on you . . .'

Olive didn't respond, couldn't. It was too early for the right words.

'Ah-hem.'

A police officer was standing in the bay window, his hat hooked under his arm. He looked awkward and fiddled with a loose strip of braid on the rim. 'Your mother has been very worried about you, young lady,' he said in a voice that was higher than Olive had expected for a man so tall. 'She's a good woman. You shouldn't have put her through this.'

'Thanks, Derek, I'll take it from here.'

'My pleasure.' The police officer scratched his head, wafting puffs of aftershave. 'Glad she's all right. Bring her down to the station tomorrow once she's had a sleep – if you're worried.'

He gave Mog a knowing look. Olive didn't need *in-tu-ition* to know that it was a knowing look.

'I'm OK, just tired.' Olive tried to smile – for Mog, strictly not for Officer Derek.

Mog looked all crumpled. 'We'll come if necessary, thanks, Derek.'

'Might see you on the other side of the bench then, Judge Garnaut.' Officer Derek popped his hat on, touched it lightly on the brim and winked. 'Glad it's all turned out.'

Once Officer Derek had shut the door, Olive looked up at Mog. 'Did you get it?'

'Yep, Olive, we did it. The Attorney-General called this morning, but in all of this hullabaloo it seems very insignificant. I have been worried sick about you – I just kept seeing your face on a milk carton.'

'They only put the faces of lost kids on milk cartons in America, Mog – in the olden days. We saw it on telly.'

Mog laughed, blew her nose on a J Cloth and tucked it back up her sleeve. Then she swivelled her head to look at the room. Olive looked, too. On top of the usual mess, there were three ashtrays on the coffee table. Butts and ash were sprinkled across everything.

'This place is a pigsty. The press are coming round at the weekend to do some "at home" shots,' said Mog.

Olive coughed. Smoke prickled her lungs. 'You'll need to air it.'

'That's what I'm worried about. I'm not sure I want this dirt aired.' Mog threw her head back and laughed heartily. Mog always laughed at her own jokes. There was something about her spirit that was so much bigger than her frame; it made people want to join in. Olive watched Mog's ribs jiggle under her top, and as Mog laughed, Olive laughed too.

Mog drew her finger through the grit that lay thick on a bookcase. 'My ideals have got in the way, Ol. They've made us dusty.'

Olive shrugged. 'Pip said you can't be a mum who makes sponge cakes *and* justice.'

Mog smiled, but it was feeble. 'Sponge cakes and

justice.' She sniffed and flicked a forthright spider from her daughter's sleeve. 'Who is this wise Pip, anyway? Maybe we can all have dinner together now that I might actually have a bit of time.'

Olive fluttered. 'How much time?'

Mog grinned. 'Frankly, I'd be happy with enough to put on a wash, but it should be even more than that. Time enough to go to the theatre this Friday night, for example. I've landed tickets to *My Fair Lady*, if you're keen.'

'Does the Rain in Spain Fall Mainly on the Plain?' Olive quoted a song from her favourite musical.

Mog drew one eyebrow into a bow, and looked down along the curve of her cheekbone. 'If you're going to use stanzas in the company of a musical-theatre tragic like your mother, darling, try to quote better songs. But yes, I expect that Every Duke and Earl and Peer will be there, and should they fail, Hugh Jackman's playing the Professor.'

Olive stuck out her tongue.

'Let's get those shoes and socks off, Ol, they're sopping. And your skirt. What have — ?'

'Hang on, there's a present for you.' Olive withdrew the wrapped frame from the top of her rucksack.

While Olive peeled back the tissue paper, Mog picked up one of the photos. 'It's the last one William took of us. That's why I look so uptight — I was doing everything I could to keep us a family.'

Olive looked at Mog and then placed the frame on Mog's lap. 'Here you go.'

'It's gorgeous!' Mog ran her finger across the loops of pips and olives, and the two fingerprints for authenticity. 'You look so happy. I'll pop it on my desk, and you can smile at me while I write my judgements.'

'That sounds pretty flash.'

Mog raised her arms and stuck out her bum in a middle-aged lawyer's take on the yoga pose 'salute the sun'.

Olive yawned, and Mog caught it. 'I may not do sponge cakes,' said Mog, 'but I can probably stretch to cocoa. Want one?'

'Yes, please.'

Mog walked slowly to the door then paused. Her sinewy hand bound the knob. 'The catch with parenting, Ol, is that it doesn't matter what a person does, how noble their intentions, they always get it wrong . . .' Her voice dribbled away and she turned into the kitchen; she was all angles, sharp and pointy.

Late into the night, Mog undressed Olive, placed a warm flannel on her face, and tucked the duvet right up tight around Olive's chin. She had made the bed with clean sheets, which were cool on Olive's legs.

Even in all that caring, though – even in clean sheets – Olive couldn't sleep. The bedroom felt strange, sparse. Olive turned to the left and then the right. Beside her, Ariel spiralled up and down the fishbowl. Somehow, her little flippy splishes only made the room emptier.

Olive sat up and hung her legs over the side of the bed. She rolled the Brass Eye between her fingers, until

231

the cylinder was sticky and her skin smelled metallic, then she slipped it into the drawer in her bedside table and stared into the fleshy black. It was curious – while there was no doubt that the room felt emptier, Olive realized that *she* did not.

Olive crept up the dark hall and into Mog's bed, just as she had as a child. Mog enfolded her in nightie warmth, and Olive snuggled back. Pressed against Mog's breast, the knick-knack dust smelled as thick and sweet as cooking cakes.

Mog squeezed Olive tight. With sleepy breath, she half croaked, half whispered, 'Don't worry, Ol, we'll get through it. We always do.'

And the funny thing was that, this time, Olive really believed her.

32
The Pip in Olive

Olive walked into Science. It was chaotic. The whole class was aware that nothing but a few paltry elements on the periodic table lay between them and a sunny afternoon. At the front of the lab, Mrs Dixon was so immersed in setting up an experiment that she was oblivious to the noise.

Olive slid in next to May in a row not too close to the front and not too close to the back (where Mathilda and Amelia were lounging). Mrs Dixon had paired Olive and May up for the last project of the year. As Olive sat down, May moved her books back onto her own bit of the bench and smiled. Olive smiled back and rubbed at a blister on her heel.

Olive had new shoes, which were destroying her feet, but they were size 5½ ladies, and even though there was some 'growing room' for summer, she was more than a little bit proud. 'It's funny the way feet grow before the rest of the body,' Mog had said when they bought them. 'Mine did that before I shot up.' Olive stretched out her legs. It was a strange thing, growing. People grew up, but they didn't dilute. The body stayed whole, solid.

Skyep walked into the lab with posture so erect she reminded Olive of those elegant African women who carry water-pots on their heads.

'What was it like?' called Amelia from the back of the room, her cheeks rosy.

'Like a slug,' said Skyep. 'It felt like someone shoving a slug in my mouth.' Unfortunately, Skyep was not always as elegant as her posture suggested.

'A slug! That's hilarious. At least you're not a kiss virgin! Come and sit here. Shove over, Till.'

Olive peered over her shoulder. There wasn't a spare seat in the back row. Mathilda looked around and moved her books into the row in front. Skyep slid in next to Amelia.

'We're all going to the wall after school if you want to come,' said Amelia. 'We're meeting James Hurley and the other Grammar boys.' As Amelia spoke, she pricked the bench with the needle point of her compass.

'Cool.' Skyep stroked a loopy gold S that dangled around her neck. Amelia looked at Skyep. Her face gleamed.

In front of them, Mathilda sat alone and glum. Olive felt a bit sorry for her, stranded in a row like that, but it was odd to think that they had once been so close. It was like the Mathilda with whom Olive had dressed up, eaten slabs of caramel slice, had baths and laughed until they were whoozy was a different Mathilda Graham altogether.

May was staring at the trio as well. 'Cycle complete.'

'What do you mean?'

'They scoop girls up and then dump them. This school can be more dangerous than Bells Beach.'

'We should cross lifesaver flags at the gates.'

May laughed.

The door banged as Nut Allergy walked into the lab, trailing papers and shoelaces. She scanned the room, but the only free seat was next to Mathilda. As Nut Allergy approached the bench, Amelia whooped. Nut Allergy concentrated on arranging her books; Mathilda went pink with shame.

Amelia leaned over her desk and poked Nut Allergy's shoulder. 'Have you got a partner for this project, Nutters?' She gestured at Mathilda and winked.

May clicked her tongue against the roof of her mouth. 'Nutters? What is it with people and names in this place?'

Nut Allergy kept her eyes on her chemistry book and spoke. 'My name is Kate.' Her words were mushroom soft.

A murmur rolled about the classroom like a Mexican wave.

Amelia snorted, sounding more horse than girl. 'Whatever, Nutters,' she said. Mathilda shifted her books further along the bench towards the wall.

'Kate strikes back,' said Olive in her new louder voice. May giggled.

Mathilda stood and the metal legs of her stool hammered the lino. 'You may be Kate at home, but you'll always be Nutters to me,' she said and winked at Amelia. 'And I'll put money on you always being a kiss virgin, too.' Mathilda fished behind her for a grin.

'Calm down, Mathilda,' said Amelia. 'It's like picking on a kid with Down's syndrome.'

Mathilda blenched.

Amelia turned away and started chatting to Skyep: conversation closed.

May raised one eyebrow at Olive in an *I-told-you* arch. 'What's with kiss virgins? Man.' She scribbled a cartoon and held it out. It was a girl with a north–south parting and a nose that was so pronounced her lips couldn't get past it. A spotty boy in school uniform looked put out. Olive laughed.

'Apparently Mathilda's mum thinks Mathilda's got a problem; that she's boy-crazy,' continued May. 'She called Stable-East about it.'

Olive rolled her eyes. 'She's certainly got problems.'

May looked up from her drawing. 'What about you? Are you boy-crazy?'

'Hardly. Boys stink like salami sandwiches left in a school bag for six weeks. You simply can't have my hygiene standards and any sort of interest in boys. With any luck, I'll be a lesbian. What about you?'

'My family . . . well, they wouldn't like that. They're not from here – they're different.'

Olive shrugged. 'Mine's weird, too.'

May looked at her.

'It's just me and Mog, my mum. We're a sort of micro-family.'

May nodded. 'I've seen your mum on the telly. What happened to your dad?'

'Dead.'

'Crap. Really?'

'Well, sort of.'

'Sort of dead?' May scrunched her nose. Olive was tempted to look her straight in the eye and tell her that Mustard Seed was actually quite dead from the knees down, but May seemed genuinely concerned. Olive twisted the cardboard casing on her rubber. 'He's not really dead. We just never had anything to do with him.'

'Oh.'

Olive shrugged. 'I guess that sometimes you can feel closer to people who aren't related than to those who are.'

'Absolutely.' May turned a page in her exercise book and nodded. 'Like me and the boarders.'

Olive peeled the cardboard back from her rubber. Under its sheath, the rubber was soft and new-white. She looked up at May. 'Would you like to come over to finish the Science project this weekend? We could go metal-detecting as well, if you like.'

'Metal-detecting?' May screeched like a kettle whistle.

Olive nodded. 'I haven't used it much yet, but it is brilliant.'

'I've always wanted to have a go at that. Apart from scratch cards, it's the only way I'm ever going to accumulate personal wealth. They should teach it in the

Business Centre instead of philanthropy – it would be so much more useful.'

Olive laughed. 'Mog can sign your pass-out if you need her to.'

'I'll get the boarding-house mistress onto it – it won't be difficult. She knows how desperate I am for home cooking.'

Although Olive hadn't really known May long, she did seem to spend a lot of time talking about her next meal. 'Home cooking for Mog extends to toast, but she'll probably take us out for lasagne, and we can always get ice cream.'

May took a muesli bar from her pencil case and broke off two hunks. 'Anything would be better than the boarding house. Friday is roast with yellow fat. I'm sure it's a breach of human rights.' She offered Olive a piece.

Olive glanced at Mrs Dixon (whose hair would have gone grey had she seen students consuming food in her lab) then shoved it in her mouth. 'Let's play the menu by ear,' she said.

May popped another clandestine chunk of muesli bar into her mouth. 'No need. I know that I will always feel like ice cream.'

'So will I – and Pip did too. Weird.' Olive blinked. It felt funny saying Pip's name like that.

May looked up. 'Who's Pip? And what's so weird?'

Olive had noticed that May did seem to be categorically into anything weird. Olive's bottom shifted on the dumpy stool and she swept a few stray oats off the bench.

'Well, what would you say if I said that once upon a time I had a sister, a twin sister, which I guess would make it *twice* upon a time.' Olive smiled. 'I don't really know where to start.'

May snorted crumbs. 'Tell me this weekend. Twice upon a time – that's quite funny.' She stopped drawing and offered Olive her notebook. 'What do you think of this one?' May held up a picture of a metal detector with an ATM sign on it.

'Now that's wicked.'

May chewed her pencil and grinned until her eyes almost disappeared.

'OK, girls. Find your seats and open your books to mercury,' said Mrs Dixon. 'Page ninety-four. Anybody know its atomic number?'

A flock of books fanned open and twenty-one out of twenty-three faces looked up. Only May's and Olive's bobs swung shiny over a cartoon hidden in the pages of 'Hg for Mercury'.

May whispered something and Olive laughed. She flung her head back and laughed so loudly that it made the girls around her want to join in. Mrs Dixon smiled. 'Olive? You are extremely jolly today. Do you know what mercury's atomic number is?'

But Olive Garnaut was laughing so heartily, she didn't even hear.

33
Footprints Tall

Late, late one evening, when distance had whittled the moon to a star, the wind whipped up. Sand blew in clouds along the shore. By morning the bluster had settled, but when the first of the fishermen wobbled down in gumboots, he stopped and looked befuddled. 'Well, squid my jig,' he chewed through a powdery mint.

The beach was smooth and unblemished but for a trail of footprints, small tracks, an older child's perhaps, heading to and then from old Kelso Pier. The scene wasn't unusual because there were footprints, however; it was unusual because the footprints stood high above the sand: size 5½ ladies' footprints, tall and proud.

Acknowledgements

At the risk of sounding last-drinks sentimental, to the following people with love and thanks . . .

My publishers Elise, Erica, Eva and Hilary at Allen & Unwin; David, Bella, Alison, Linda, Hannah and Tiffany at David Fickling Books; and Doubleday Canada, together with my agents, Pippa Masson and Marie Campbell – all of whom have worked so very hard to support somebody so very new.

My mother, who has so much to offer and offered it first to her family (and for saying *restaurong* like the French).

My father, who has a delicious sense of humour, a clear mind, an enviable work ethic – and a scalpel named after him to prove it.

My witty and talented siblings, T and Jamie-Kane (who have threatened to write their memoirs).

My grandmother, Nen, the healthiest, fittest, most elegant little-old-lady in the country, and her great-grandson, Angus King, just because.

To J and Eva (because every family needs a brain surgeon and a German).

For all the people in my classes at RMIT who suggested there was no place for the original final chapter in this novel. For Clare Renner – the Ms Chips of children's lit – who insisted on it.

For Lisa, Ports, Lizzie and my-May, who read late drafts and provided counselling/coffee/very thoughtful comments.

For Sof, Kristen, Grot, Kate, Priya-my-writing-partner, Meg, Lee, Stacey, Jess and Rayment, all of whom read (various) early drafts. To Tone, who didn't, but still had an opinion.

To Elise Hurst, for her perfect cover illustration.

To Steve Merson, Archivist at Lighthouses of Victoria Inc, who so graciously answered my questions and who is not in any way responsible for my creative inter-pretations of his facts.

To the Hathaway-haters and Guinnerang, for their enthusiasm, combined sense of direction and very fine company.

And finally, to my colleagues at UGL, who have been so supportive of the part-time position and who laugh at (most of) my jokes.

That does not really leave a lot of mystique, but luckily I'm not that kind of person.

* Mog Garnaut would like to acknowledge José Saramago's novel, *The Double*, which she very much enjoyed.